LILY'S LUCK

Land Run Mail-Order Brides (Book 10)

Bestselling and Award-Winning Author

NANCY FRASER

This is a work of fiction. Names, characters, places and incidents are either the product of the author's imagination or are used fictitiously, and any resemblance to actual persons living or dead, business establishments, events, or locales, is entirely coincidental.

Lily's Luck
Land Run Mail-Order Brides – Book 10

COPYRIGHT © 2022 by Nancy Fraser

Books From a Romantic's Heart Publishing
Contact Information:
romwriter96(at)gmail(dot)com

Cover by Black Widow Books © 2022

About the Oklahoma Land Run of April, 1892

The third land run began at high noon on April 19, 1892 into the lands (4,300,000 acres) of the Cheyenne and Arapaho. Blaine, Dewey, Day, Roger Mills, Custer and Washita Counties date their beginnings from this homestead run of approximately 25,000 citizens.

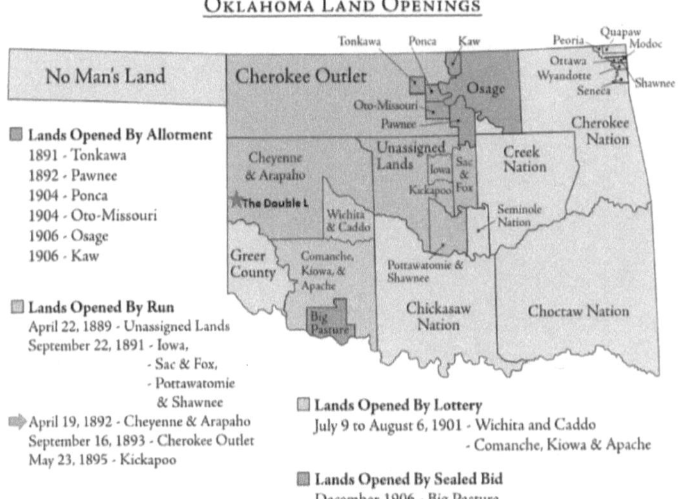

Chapter One

Winter Cotillion
Hildebrand House
Boston Area Known as Back Bay
February 12, 1892

Lily Marie O'Halloran turned full-circle in the ornate ballroom of the newly built home belonging to Arthur Hildebrand, one of Boston's most prominent businessmen. As lovely as her own Beacon Hill home was, Hildebrand House was exquisite.

The marble floors glistened. Despite being trod upon by a huge number of Boston elite who had turned out for the winter cotillion. Chandeliers fitted with Mister Edison's electric candles glowed brightly above the crowd.

"Isn't it absolutely beautiful?" Cassie, Lily's younger sister, commented.

"Yes," Lily confirmed. "Lovely indeed." She scanned the room one last time before adding, "Mister Hildebrand has definitely outdone everyone with this fancy new home."

"Do you suppose William will be here?" Cassie asked. "I know he's away at university, but I thought—"

"According to mother, the entire Hildebrand family will be in attendance." Beneath her breath, Lily muttered, "Unfortunately."

Cassie swatted playfully at Lily's arm. "Don't be like that. I know you tire of mother's matchmaking efforts, but would it be so horrible to marry into such an affluent family?"

"I'm happy to leave that honor to you and Becca. After all, there are only two sons, so it stands to reason the two of you, at eighteen and twenty, would be far more suitable matches."

"But you should marry first," Cassie insisted.

Lily let loose a most unladylike snort of laughter. "It's sweet of you to think so, Cassie. But, at twenty-six, I'm a bit too far on the shelf. Any man of means or breeding isn't going to want to stake his future on me."

"But Rupert is at least six years older than you. Surely, he wouldn't be put off by your age. You're beautiful, talented—you play the piano far better than Becca and me—and you're smart."

"And, as our mother so often likes to point out, I'm also opinionated, outspoken, and a pain in the bustle. Not that I would wear one of those foul contraptions."

"Speaking of mother," Cassie whispered, "here

she comes, with Mister Hildebrand and Rupert in tow."

The three of them came to a stop in front of Lily and Cassie. Rupert bowed at the waist, and lifted both Cassie's and Lily's fingers to his lips for a brief kiss. "Good evening, ladies. Are you enjoying yourselves so far?"

"Everything is lovely," Cassie gushed.

"Very nice," Lily agreed. "I do believe the majority of Boston proper are in attendance."

"Exactly as I'd planned," Arthur Hildebrand bragged, his gaze raking her from head-to-toe as he spoke. "There's no sense owning such a fine home if you're not going to show it off."

Wanting to escape the strange way Mister Hildebrand was leering at her, Lily turned to her mother and asked, "Where's papa and Becca? I haven't seen them since we arrived."

Eleanor O'Halloran swept her arm wide, encompassing the whole of the massive ballroom. "Your father is doing his duty by chaperoning your sister while she's out on the ballroom floor with Mister William Hildebrand.

At Lily's side, Cassie gave a soft whimper. Cassie had been head-over-heels for the youngest Hildebrand son since they first met summer before last at the Hildebrand's lakeside vacation home.

Obviously, her mother's matchmaking efforts had paired up the wrong daughter with the soon-to-be solicitor.

Rupert settled his dark gaze on Cassie, totally oblivious to her distress. "Miss Cassandra, I was hoping I could escort you to the dancefloor as well."

Cassie recovered quickly. Blinking back any show of upset, she flashed Rupert a demure smile. "I'd be delighted."

Lily's breath came out on a sigh of relief. While she felt bad for her sister, the realization that the eldest Hildebrand son had set his cap for Cassie rather than her, made Lily immensely happy. Rupert was all right, she supposed, but she felt nothing other than a passing friendship toward the man.

He was definitely handsome. Successful. Poised to take over the family business some day, he was most assuredly a fine catch. Assuming a woman was interested only in the trappings of an arranged marriage. Lily, had no such interest. She preferred to remain single her entire life rather than marry for money, position, or to avoid being labeled a spinster.

"They make a striking couple, don't they?" Her mother's question was aimed directly at Arthur Hildebrand.

The widower nodded his agreement, then

focused his attention back on Lily. "What do you think, Miss O'Halloran? Is a match between Rupert and Miss Cassandra, and my younger son William and Miss Rebecca, not an excellent arrangement for both our families?"

"I suppose," Lily agreed grudgingly. "Despite the fact that arranged marriages went out with the Victorian bathwater."

"Lily Marie!" Eleanor scolded.

Much to Lily's and her mother's surprise, the senior Hildebrand broke into laughter. "I'd heard you were outspoken, Miss Lily, but I believe this is the first time I've been witness to your refreshing honesty."

"And I'm most appreciative of the fact you weren't offended, sir," Lily told him. "I get so tired of apologizing."

"At fifty-five, I'm far too old... too experienced... to be easily offended." Turning toward her mother, he added, "I believe our previous discussion—your suggestion—is perfectly acceptable and exactly what I need."

A knot twisted inside her gut, but Lily dared to ask, "What suggestion?"

Her mother lifted Lily's hands in hers and squeezed tightly. "A match of course. Between you, our eldest daughter, and Mister Arthur Hildebrand."

Lily's gaze shot from her mother to the widower and back again. "Have you lost your mind, mother?" Biting her lip, she offered, "Again, no offense intended, Mister Hildebrand, but I've no intention of marrying a man old enough to be my father."

His steely gray stare narrowed in her direction. "I guarantee you, young lady, I'm still in the prime of my life for the more important aspects in a marital relationship."

Lily swallowed the lump forming in her throat and gave a sound shake of her head. "I truly don't know what to say. Other than *absolutely not*." Swiveling around, she made a dash for the closest door. Over her shoulder, she called out, "I'll hire a ride home, mother. Stay and enjoy your triumph in matching your two youngest daughters."

Thirty minutes later, Lily was rushing through the door of her Beacon Hill home and up the stairs to her corner bedroom. Emmaline, her lady's maid, followed closely behind.

"Miss Lily, what's the matter? Why are you home so early, and by yourself?"

"I had to get out of there," she insisted. "My mother was about to marry me off, and I couldn't stand being there for another moment."

The young maid pursed her lips in an obvious effort to hold in her laughter. Lily was not as easily amused. Having been her maid for nearly a decade, Emmaline had been a witness to all of Lily's previous matchmaking disasters.

"I know your mother can be pushy, Miss Lily, but she has your best interests at heart. She wants to see you married and settled into your own home. To have your own family." Almost as an afterthought, she asked, "Who was it this time? Rupert Hildebrand? Or, were her sights set on another of the Boston upper crust?"

"Oh, much, much worse," Lily said, not waiting for Emmaline's help in shrugging out of her fancy ballgown. "She all but promised me to Arthur Hildebrand."

"Old man Hildebrand," Emmaline gasped. "He's old enough to be your father."

"Exactly what I told them. Just before I fled the party."

"While I can certainly understand your reluctance in this instance, you know she's not going to stop until she's found you a husband."

"I've got to get out of here. Not just this house, but all of Boston. I've got money, thanks to my inheritance from Nana Watson. Perhaps, I'll go to Chicago."

"And what would you do once you're there?" Emmaline asked. "It's not as if you've got any special training, other than time spent at that snobby finishing school, and being a high society debutante."

Lily rolled her eyes and shrugged her shoulders, letting the honesty of her maid's assessment sink in. "I'm smart, as my darling sister pointed out earlier tonight. I can learn anything I need to in order to get by. You could come with me. At my expense, of course."

Emmaline shook her head. "No, thank you. I appreciate the offer, but I've met someone and we've become close. He's a foreman at the textile factory, a hardworking and good man. I'm hoping he'll ask for my hand."

"How wonderful," Lily told her honestly. "I wish you the best, of course."

"If you're serious about escaping your family home, what about something a little farther west?"

"How much farther?" Lily asked, a bit apprehensive yet curious.

"My cousin Pearl recently exchanged letters with a company that places mail order brides with men out west."

"A mail order bride? I'd be leaving one untenable situation for another."

"That's the beauty of this particular matching service," Emmaline explained. "You don't have to make a match until you meet the person up front. At the moment, they're looking for woman who are willing to marry and take part in the next Oklahoma Land Run in April."

"Land run? You mean where they race across barren countryside in search of a spot to homestead?"

Emmaline nodded vigorously, obviously caught up in her own suggestion. "It's all so romantic, if you think about it. Going into the unknown with a man you've just met and married." Helping Lily out of her petticoats, Emmaline reminded her, "You're the one who's always saying how you crave adventure, rather than a mundane life as a Boston socialite. Now's your chance. Assuming you really meant what you said."

Lily settled herself in at her dressing table and handed Emmaline her hairbrush. Closing her eyes, she let the rhythm of the soft bristles being drawn through her long red tresses relax her.

After a few moments, she asked, "Exactly what would I have to do to get in on this grand adventure."

"From what I remember in the flyer Pearl received, you send in your name and particulars like height and weight, a photograph, and answer some questions about health. They even have a spot on the form for you to write down you'd want in a husband. It's almost as if you'd be looking for a mail order groom."

A mail order groom? Lily held up her hand and touched the tip of one finger with her thumb. "He'd have to be a Christian, of course." Ticking off the next finger, she continued. "He should be my age or a few years older, but not *old* old."

"A hard worker would be good," Emmaline said, her suggestion causing Lily to tap a third finger.

"He has to have a vision for his... our... future. Not just someone who wants to grab a plot of land with no idea what to do with it."

Giggling, Emmaline, added, "Handsome and tall with big hands."

"Big hands?"

A second giggle escaped, but Emmaline tamped it down. "Never mind. It's not important."

Lily wasn't so sure. Something about the man having 'big hands' had certainly set off Emmaline's girlish side.

"How do I get the application?" Lily asked. Surely it wouldn't hurt to have a look.

"I'll see if Pearl has a spare. I know they sent her a few, no doubt hoping she has friends who might be interested."

"I'm not saying I'm going to fill it out, of course,

but it would be interesting to take a peek at what they're offering."

"Exactly," Emmaline agreed. Setting the brush aside, she stepped back and reached for Lily's nightdress. "Let's get you out of that corset and into bed before your parents get home. I can tell them you retired early with a headache. That way, you can put off your mother's rant until morning."

"You're the sweetest, Emmaline. I truly hope your young man realizes how special you are and offers you a ring."

"One thing's for certain, Miss Lily, if I can get you squared away first—even if it means sending you off a train headed west—it'll make leaving my employ a whole lot easier."

Lily sank into the plush mattress of her huge, canopy bed, and drew the silky covers up to her chin. Yes, she had told Emmaline—and anyone else who would listen—that she craved adventure. If traveling by train to Wichita, meeting and marrying a perfect stranger, and setting out across barren land formerly belonging to one of the many Indian tribes was what it took to slake her thirst for excitement, then so be it.

She couldn't very well claim to want something so desperately and then be too cowardly to follow through. *Could she?*

Chapter Two

MacKinnon Acres
Cottonwood Falls, Kansas
Early April, 1892

Brendan MacKinnon removed the last of his personal belongings from the farmhouse where he'd grown up, and set them inside the Conestoga wagon he'd purchased just two days earlier. Raised by his uncle after his parents perished in a fire, he'd lived on this homestead since he was six. Leaving would definitely be bittersweet.

As of earlier this week, the thriving wheat and barley farm had been sold to someone else, and he was on his way to Oklahoma in hopes of becoming what he truly wanted to be. A cattleman.

All he needed was a parcel of land and a partner. Someone to share his dreams and—if his plan panned out—his life. The idea had come to him like a vision from the Almighty. At twenty-nine, he needed a wife and eventually—should the Lord see fit—a family of his own. Hopefully, the mail order bride service he'd contacted could make good on their promises and provide him with a suitable woman to share his vision.

He had a little more than a week to make his way to Wichita in time for what they were calling their 'matching day'. The whole thing was designed so perspective grooms could meet the women anxious to wed and accompany their new husband on the upcoming land run. Absently, Bren wondered how many of these women would be as eager once they found out exactly what he had in mind.

Farming was one thing. Ranching on previously untried land was quite another. The chance of failure, far greater.

Pete Waters, an old friend of his late uncle's, had made the run in '89 and settled on a nice parcel in the unassigned lands of the Oklahoma Territory. The stories he'd written about in his letters had fueled Bren's imagination. Now, with his uncle gone, he had no reason not to follow through with his imaginings.

He felt confident in where he wanted to stake his claim, of how he intended to circumvent the usual route to get there first, and of exactly how he'd map out his land. What he wasn't as confident about was finding the right woman.

First and foremost, she should be a good Christian. She needed to be healthy, of sturdy mind and body. His desired wife should be a good cook, and a hard worker who didn't mind getting her hands dirty. No frilly women need apply.

It would also help if she wasn't squeamish about fulfilling her wifely duties. Not that he would ever force himself on her, if she were unwilling, but he had every intention of making their marriage complete in all senses of the word. Including having a family.

Bren climbed onto the bench seat of his wagon and cast one last glance at the old homestead. With a snap of the reins, he set the pair of strong draft horses in motion, his handsome gelding tethered to the back. He was finally on his way to the starting point for the run and this next phase of his life with an excitement he hadn't felt in years.

It was half-past seven the evening of the sixteenth when Bren pulled his wagon into place in the open field at the starting line for the upcoming run. He checked in at the organizer's table and received the information he'd need for how he was to stake his claim. He was given six cloth flags with his assigned number stitched into the material, as well as a map with the plot locations and numbers listed in order.

"Spend the next couple of days going over the rules," the man at the table told him. "You can read, can't you?"

"Of course I can read. I can write, too." Shooting the man a grin, he added, "I also play the banjo, and I'm told I'm a passable square dancer."

The man who'd identified himself just as Zeke, snorted a laugh. "Well then, young fellow, you're sure to be the pick of the crop at Missus Miller's get together tomorrow night, aren't ya?"

"It's me who'll be doing the picking," Bren said with confidence. "However, I suppose it wouldn't hurt to get a haircut and shave."

"The barber shop opens at eight in the morning. You'll find it on the main road, just two doors down from the saloon. Are you boarding your horses at the livery?"

"Yes, I was hoping to. I want to make sure they're in top shape for the run."

"Cyrus is still there, if you want to lead them over. The boarding house has a couple rooms left."

"I was hoping I could sleep in my wagon, rather than wasting money on a room."

Zeke spat a wad of tobacco on the ground at his side, and then explained, "You're welcome to sleep wherever you want. However, if you happen to catch yourself a willing woman at the mixer, she might not want to spend her wedding night in the back of a dirty old wagon."

"You got a point there, Zeke," Bren agreed.

"Maybe I could arrange a hotel room for the night of the eighteenth, assuming we get hitched that morning."

"Or, if'n you find yourself a woman with some experience under her belt, she might not care when or where she consummates the marriage."

"I suppose there's that," he conceded. "To tell the truth, I've been so consumed with plotting out my run, I hadn't given the wedding night all that much thought."

"Can I give you word of advice?" Zeke asked.

"As long as it's free."

"Don't go proposing to the first filly you see. Take your time and make sure she's what you want. Or, as close as you can get."

"I'll do my best. Thanks for the words of wisdom."

"Ain't no wisdom about it, son, just practicality. I went for the first pretty one I saw and, now on twenty years later, all I got to show for it is a cranky old woman who does nothing but harp on me and spend my hard-earned money."

"So, I shouldn't look for pretty?"

"If you can find one, I suppose it would be okay as long as there's more to her than just looks."

"I got it covered, old man. I know exactly what I'm looking for in a wife. I just hope Missus Miller can make good on her word of someone for everyone."

Somewhere East of Kansas City, Kansas
April 17, 1892

Lily shifted nervously on the padded seat in the first class section of the train. They were running late after being stalled by a freakishly late snowfall when they came through Illinois.

The train was supposed to stop in Kansas City early in the morning of the seventeenth. Then, continue on to Wichita and arrive in enough time for her to claim a room at the local hotel. She'd hoped to be able to freshen up before going to the scheduled party hosted by Missus Miller and her matrimonial service.

Now, here it was half past two in the afternoon and they still had a few more hours of travelling to go. She'd be lucky, she realized, to have time to drop off her two carpet bags and change out of her traveling suit before she was due at the get-together.

Deep down, there was a part of her that wished to miss the event. She still couldn't believe she was about to do something so daring. The idea of being put on display as a possible bride for a complete stranger was sending flutters to the very pit of her stomach.

Perhaps it was fate that the train had been delayed. Maybe it was a sign from the Almighty that she wasn't supposed to become someone's wife. *At least not without love.*

"Excuse me, Miss," the porter said quietly, drawing her from her thoughts. "We're still at least an hour from Kansas City, and then another two to Wichita. If you'd like to go back to your cabin and relax for a bit, I can send an attendant to let you know when we're close."

"Thank you, but I'm fine here. If it weren't for the fact that I'm on a tight schedule for the evening, I'd truly be able to appreciate this beautiful scenery."

The man gave a nod of his head and backed away, leaving Lily to return to her thoughts. Her recent memories. Her mother had been livid when she'd told her parents she was leaving home and traveling west to make a new life for herself.

'What about your sisters? What will happen to their intended matches if you insult Mister Hildebrand by refusing his proposal?'

Eleanor O'Halloran's temper tantrum had fallen on deaf ears. Lily would no longer allow herself to be brow beaten by her mother's attempt to climb even higher on the Boston social register.

Yet, for all her bravado, she'd nearly backed out of her planned trip. Not that she would have accepted marriage to the senior Hildebrand, no matter what. Then, two days before she was scheduled to leave, her father had finally spoken up.

'Go, Lily Marie, with my blessing. You're worth so much more than being Arthur Hildebrand's newest acquisition. Take that adventure you've always wanted. Just promise me, you'll write and let us know where you've finally settled.'

So, here she was, at least three hours away from either becoming someone's intended, or upchucking all over the man's boots and scaring him away. Or, worse case scenario, not being chosen and having to fend for herself in a new and unfamiliar city. Not that she would mind if that happened. After all, it wasn't as if she would be destitute if she didn't marry. She could find a place to live, get a job, make a life for herself.

Perhaps you should have taken a few cooking lessons like Emmaline had suggested. Maybe learned how to do laundry, or how to sew something other than tatting lace or embroidery.

About the only advice she had taken to heart was to leave behind the majority of her fancy wardrobe in favor of more practical dresses and a couple of pairs of riding trousers and simple shirts. Other than her blue evening dress and the white dress she'd selected for her possible wedding day, for all intents and purposes, she looked like any ordinary woman rather than a rich man's spoiled, eldest daughter.

Hopefully, that would be enough to attract an honest and kind man.

"Welcome to the Wichita's Grand Hotel, Miss O'Halloran," the young man greeted. "When we received news of the railway delay, we held onto a few extra rooms. I can have a man take your bags up, if you'd like to head on over to the main salon. Missus Miller's get-to-know-you event is still going on for another hour or so."

"Do you know if there are any couples remaining to be matched?" She felt foolish asking. Yet, if there were no possible matches left, what would be the sense of even bothering to attend?

"To be honest, there have been a dozen or so couples come out together. The circuit judge and at least one of the local ministers were busy marrying them off in the room we decorated for the occasion." Sparing her a smile, he told her, "There were twenty-four men and twenty-two women who arrived for the party, so there must be some left." He paused, and met her gaze. "If I might be so bold, I wouldn't worry none if I were you. The moment you walk into the room, you're going to be surrounded by hopeful men."

Offering a demure smile, she said softly, "Thank you."

"The only problem you may run into will be if there are any men you might want to marry."

She swallowed away the dryness in her throat. "Late comers can't be choosers."

"I suppose," he agreed. "However, take your time. Most of the women in there have been to the well and back a few times, or aren't married for one reason or another. My guess is you're still single by choice."

"Something like that," she said, laughing.

Pulling in a deep breath to calm her nerves, she stepped away from the front desk and smoothed the wrinkles out of her staid traveling suit. A quick brush of her hand across her tightly coiled hair was all the fussing she could manage. Everything as neatly in place as possible, she began the long walk down the hallway toward what might possibly be the biggest mistake she'd ever made.

Chapter Three

Bren stood off to the side of the nearly-empty room. There were less than a dozen people left, five women and six men by his count. The men were all considerably older than his twenty-nine years. Unfortunately, so were the women.

Two widows with grown children, two former saloon workers, and a very stark looking schoolmarm. At least that's what the listing he'd been given said. Given there were two names on the list that hadn't shown up, Bren couldn't help but wonder if they'd met earlier and decided to skip the whole greeting process.

The entryway door opened, the loud click drawing his attention, as well as that of every other person in the room. The woman who stepped through was tall, slim, and at least a dozen years younger than any of her counterparts.

He pushed himself away from the wall and joined the queue of men who'd also noticed the late arrival. Picking up his speed, he closed the distance between them a half-dozen long strides.

Lily O'Halloran. The name badged pinned to the bodice of her stark brown jacket listed her age as twenty-six. She glanced from side-to-side, offering each of the men before her a cautious smile. The closer Bren got, the more he realized she was as nervous as he was—her eyes wide with fear—her pulse beating rapidly at the side of her long, elegant throat.

Bren's breath hitched. Her skin—what little he could see of it in her buttoned-up suit—was like alabaster. Obviously, Miss O'Halloran wasn't used to working in the sun. If her delicate hands were anything to go by, she probably hadn't done a hard day's work in her life either.

Definitely *not* what he was looking for in a wife, a partner. Still, he couldn't help himself when his turn came for an introduction.

"Mister Brendan MacKinnon," Missus Miller began, "may I introduce Miss Lily Marie O'Halloran from Boston."

Bren brushed his hand across the leg of his trousers and offered it to her. "Hello, Miss O'Halloran. It's nice to make your acquaintance."

She placed her hand in his, the touch of her soft skin sending his senses sideways.

"It's lovely to meet you too, Mister MacKinnon."

"Would you like some punch?" he asked, the simple words tangling on his tongue.

"No, but thank you for offering. I'd much prefer

to talk, if you've got a few minutes."

"I've got all the time you need."

She gave him a coy smile that set his heart pounding.

"Good. I guess, first of all, I should ask—what are looking for in a wife?"

Bren did his best to recall the long list of attributes he'd thought of the day before, but all that currently came to mind was tall, redheaded, with skin as soft as a newborn lamb. Swallowing back the sudden dryness in his throat, he told her, "Obviously, someone who doesn't mind marrying a total stranger." Once the first sentence came out, mostly in some semblance of order, he relaxed a bit and added, "Someone who doesn't mind the thought of taking part in the land run over rugged territory. A woman who can handle hard work, can cook a decent meal over a campfire, and..."

His words stalled when her complexion paled, the slight change accentuating a spray of freckles across her high cheekbones.

Why hadn't he noticed those before? The cheekbones, and the freckles.

"Have I said something wrong?" he asked.

She shook her head, the tightly coiled hair she'd pinned at her nape coming loose enough to send a few stray tendrils flying across her cheeks. The beat of his heart picked up speed.

"No, of course not. It's just that your list is far longer than the few men in line ahead of you."

Her honesty drew his laugh. "I'd reckon those old codgers would say almost anything to get a young woman like you into their bed." He immediately regretted the insensitive remark when her face flushed a bright shade of pink. "My apologies. That was rude. I'm truly sorry."

"Is it rude and insensitive of me to say I agree with you?"

There it was again, her unbridled truthfulness. An attribute he'd not even put on his list, but one he truly valued. "How about you, Miss O'Halloran? What are you looking for in a husband?"

She made a show of glancing around at the men who now stood off to the side, their narrowed stares shooting daggers in his direction.

"Someone far closer to my age than those fellows." She raised her head, meeting his gaze. "Your age, perhaps. Also, a man who has a plan for this land run over and above just staking his claim to a piece of the Almighty's fine earth."

His offered her a tentative smile. "That would be me, then. I'm planning to become a cattleman. I even know exactly which section of land I want, and why."

"You've obviously put some thought into your plan. I like that. The only other things I need in a husband include him being a kind and honest Christian man." She paused, as if gauging his reaction, then added, "It would also be helpful if he wasn't absolutely set on those cooking skills you mentioned."

"Something tells me, Lily Marie O'Halloran, that I'd find it most pleasurable teaching you to cook."

Her coy smile came again. And, as it had before, it nearly undid what little was left of his composure.

At ten-thirty the next morning, Lily stood nervously in front of the dressing mirror in her hotel room. Her hands trembling, she smoothed out the skirt of her white eyelet lace dress and ran her fingers through her loosely pinned curls, letting the full weight of her long hair flow freely down her back.

This was it. She was about to become Missus Brendan MacKinnon. Wife of a would-be cattleman. The realization of what she was about to do both excited and frightened her in equal measure.

They'd left the mixer together last night after signing Missus Miller's standard set of forms. Bren—as he preferred to be called—had paid the required fee, even though she'd offered to pay half. Then, he'd escorted her to her hotel room and left her there to return to his wagon. Just the memory of his lips against the backs of her fingers—as he'd bid her goodnight—made her breath catch.

Lily cast one final glance at the broach watch she'd laid on the nearby table. The minister was due to arrive at the hotel in fifteen minutes. With three other couples yet to be married, she and Mister MacKinnon were the last in line. Theirs would be a simple ceremony, fifteen minutes or less. Yet, the vows were being said before a man of the cloth, rather than a judge. An arrangement they'd both insisted on.

Promptly at eleven, a knock sounded at her door.

"Oh, my dear, you look lovely," Missus Miller said, pushing her way into the room. "Are you ready to get hitched?"

Lily nodded and licked her dry lips. "Yes, I am. I think."

Elvira Miller chuckled. "You'll be fine, dearie. I see this match as a sign the Almighty was looking out for you and Mister MacKinnon."

"A sign? What kind of sign?" Lily asked, a sudden rush of nerves nearly buckling her knees.

"The good kind, Miss O'Halloran. It was most

fortunate that your intended was so fussy and unwilling to settle on an unsuitable match just for the sake of getting married. And, equally lucky for you that you arrived late. Had you gotten here on time, you may have missed him in the crowd and chosen someone else." Elvira straightened her shoulders, her large bosom lifting with pride. "Dare I say it, you two are the most suited out of all the couples in this latest crop of hopeful matches. Quite possibly the best match I've facilitated so far."

"How can you possibly tell that by knowing us less than a day?"

"Let's just say, I've got an eye for these things." Holding Lily's shawl for her, Missus Miller offered, "Is there anything you'd like to ask? You know, about the wedding night and all?"

"No, thank you," Lily responded, the warm flush of her skin telling her she was likely a red as the color of her hair. "Our mother was always upfront with us girls about what to expect in the marriage bed."

"Well, that's refreshing. It's been my experience that most mothers shy away from the more intimate details."

"Not mine. She told us all about a man's urges, and our duty as wives."

The woman nearly choked on another laugh.

"Urges? Duty? My word!"

Lily swallowed and met the woman's broad grin. "They don't have urges? Or demand to claim their rights?"

"Oh, they have urges alrighty. Often, if you're lucky. However, a good man doesn't demand. He woos and excites his woman. He treats her with respect while still making her want him as much as he wants her."

"What... um... what kind of a man do you think Mister MacKinnon will be?"

"That young buck? My guess is, he's a wooer, and definitely a man who could rise to the occasion and create some powerful excitement."

"What if I can't... I mean... what if—"

"Oh, pshaw, dearie. You'll be fine. You just need to relax. Let your man do the work in the beginning until you're comfortable."

"I can do that," she confirmed, albeit somewhat reluctantly.

"Of course, you can. Now, let's get you downstairs so you can claim that handsome devil for your own."

Lily took a moment to think about her future husband. Yes, indeed, he was handsome, with chestnut hair that hung to just below his ears, warm brown eyes that darkened when he stared at her. He was tall, at least six-two, which meant she could wear her button shoes with the heels and not be towering over him. He'd been clean shaven last night, yet she wondered what he'd look like with the scruff of a day old beard. Pulling herself from her thoughts, she responded, "He is rather nice looking, isn't he?"

"That he is. Why do you think those women were hovering around him like flies on a mule? All that matters though, is that you two chose each other."

"Yes, I suppose it is. I just hope he's not as nervous as I am."

"Dearie, when he gets one look at you, all gussied up for your wedding day, he'll forget all about nerves. Chances are, he'll also want to forget about the big luncheon we got planned and suggest making a beeline back up here to this room."

Adamantly, Lily shook her head. "No. Lunch first, followed maybe by a walk and a tour of his traveling wagon."

"You say that now, but you'll soon change your tune. Marriage, and all that comes with it, will come naturally."

Lily hoped it were so. Yet, when the woman opened the door and ushered her out into the long hallway, all Lily could think about was turning tail and running in the opposite direction.

Bren stood at the makeshift altar in the front of the sparsely decorated room. Small vases of flowers sat alongside a dozen or so chairs creating an aisleway for the bride to walk along on her way to meet her groom. He'd taken one of the seats just twenty minutes before and watched as a very nervous looking young man, probably in his mid-twenties, shuffled from foot-to-foot beside the preacher. The bride, a good ten years older than her groom, had sidled down the aisle as if she were going to a dance, her broad grin showing tobacco-stained teeth.

It was then that Bren realized he'd dodged a bullet. Patience, his uncle had always said, would pay off in the long run. He'd never paid much attention to his uncle's words of wisdom until now. Until he'd passed on the first batch of woman, and Lily O'Halloran had bewitched him into taking a wife not at all like what he'd thought he wanted.

Near the back of the room, a middle-aged woman in a flowered hat took her seat at the piano and began playing a familiar hymn. The minister leaned in Bren's direction and asked, "Are you ready to take your vows, young man?"

Bren sucked in a breath. "As ready as I'll ever be, I suppose."

The man gave a nod and the double doors opened wide. Lily stepped across the threshold, the very sight of her causing the breath he'd drawn to rush out of his lungs all at once. At his side, the minister smothered a chuckle.

Dressed in a white lacy dress, her long red hair pulled back in loose curls around her face and hanging freely across her slim shoulders, Lily looked totally different than she had the night before. Last night, she'd looked all prim and proper in her staid traveling suit. Today, she looked like a sweet, young innocent. A temptation.

She was beautiful. And she was about to become his wife.

Chapter Four

"And do you, Lily Marie O'Halloran, take Brendan David MacKinnon to be your lawfully wedded husband?"

The minister's question echoed in Lily's ears, the very import of her impending answer making her dizzy. Raising her head, she fixed her gaze on Bren. "I do," she responded.

Bren's sigh of obvious relief feathered across her cheek. His fingers tightened around hers.

"Do you have a ring?" Reverend Marshall asked.

"Yes," Bren confirmed, releasing her hand long enough to dig into his vest pocket. When he unfurled his fingers, two plain gold bands lay in his open palm.

She lifted her trembling hand higher so he could slide the ring in place. Then, she took the other ring from his grasp and slid it in place on his left hand.

The reverend smiled down at them, and said solemnly, "By the power vested in my by the Almighty above, and the great state of Kansas, I now pronounce you husband and wife." He paused for a brief moment, and then added, "You may now kiss your bride."

When Bren leaned forward, Lily drew in a quick breath. He pressed his mouth gently against hers, the warmth of his kiss making her insides flutter.

And that was it. They were married.

Bren closed his hand around hers and led her away from the altar and down the aisle until they were outside the makeshift wedding chapel.

"Well, Missus MacKinnon," he said, a subdued grin lifting the corners of his full lips. "Should we join the other happy couples at the luncheon?" When she didn't respond immediately, he reached out and lifted her chin on the tips of his fingers until their gazes locked. "Or, if you'd rather, we can take that tour of my wagon set up, and get a meal on our own at the local café."

"Yes, please. I think spending the afternoon getting to know one another better would be far preferable to sharing a meal with a bunch of strangers. Especially given, as of tomorrow at noon, those same couples will be doing their best to leave us behind in their dust."

He offered her his arm. "We'll be going over to the open field where the wagons are parked, and stopping by the livery, if you'd prefer to change out of your beautiful dress."

Shaking her head, she told him, "It's not every day a woman gets to wear her wedding dress. I'm fine like this a while longer."

As if he could sense her hesitation, he told her, "You don't need to worry, Lily. I don't intend to pounce on you the minute we return to your... our... hotel room."

Sighing softly, she told him, "I wasn't worried—"

"You weren't?" Bren asked, a muscle twitching in his firm jaw. To his credit, he didn't laugh at her.

"Well, I'm not worried that you'd force me or anything, but I do admit to being nervous." She offered him what she hoped was a brave smile, and admitted, "Very nervous."

Tugging gently on their joined arms, he steered them toward a remote corner of the hotel lobby. "I've been thinking about our wedding night."

"You have?"

"As matter of fact, it kept me up most of last night." He pulled in a breath, and told her, "If you'd like to wait before we... um... before we consummate the marriage, I'm fine with that. We could wait until after we've claimed our homestead. That'll give us a few more days to get to know one another better."

"Is..." Her words stalled. Embarrassment flooded her cheeks with heat. "Is that what you want? To wait?"

A low growl, mixed with a chuckle, escaped his throat. "Any man in his right mind wouldn't wait before taking you to his bed."

She bit back a laugh, and asked, "So, are you saying you're insane?"

As he'd done before, he lifted her chin with his gentle touch. Leaning forward, he pressed his lips to hers. Only this time, it wasn't the chaste kiss he'd given her at the end of their ceremony. He leaned into the kiss, increasing the pressure, the very weight of his mouth against hers making her heart pound, and the dizziness return.

When he broke the kiss and raised his head, he told her, "I'm not crazy, but I am patient. I've no intention of making a mistake in this marriage, so you hold all the cards as to when and where we first make love."

"Oh..." She licked her lips and Bren's dark eyes widened. Lily swallowed back the dryness in her throat, and admitted, "I've never... I mean..."

He smoothed the pad of his thumb across her lower lip. "I assumed as much, Lily. Or, at least I hoped so. However, if I wasn't your first, it wouldn't have mattered."

"Have you? Ever?"

Bren took her hand in his and led her out of the corner and toward the front door of the hotel. She wondered if he was avoiding her question. *Had she embarrassed him by asking?*

Once they'd reached the brick sidewalk that ran along the main street of town, he leaned close to her side and told her, "Yes, I have. Not in a while, but I have."

"That's a relief," she said, releasing the breath she held.

His laugh was full, and delightful. "Come on, Missus MacKinnon. Let's go take a look at the close quarters we'll be sharing for the next few weeks."

"Weeks?"

"I figure it'll take us three days to reach the plot of land I intend to claim. After that, we'll have to build a house. Like it or not, my wagon is going to be home until we're done."

Bren tightened his grip around Lily's hand. When they came to the end of the walkway, he stepped off the curb and guided her down to the dirt road. He wasn't sure what he was expecting when he decided to throw his hat in the ring for a wife, but it definitely wasn't Lily.

It was obvious she was gently raised. Delicate. Yet, obviously daring to have left the comfort of her east coast home in search of not only a land run adventure, but also marriage to a stranger. She was also intelligent and had done her research about what was involved in the government's land run.

They reached the first of three big fields where at least a couple dozen wagons were parked. The local sheriff's office patrolled the area from time to time, and at least one of the organizers were there around the clock to make sure there was no vandalism. He'd had to show his registration papers last night just to be allowed to spend the night with his wagon and supplies.

"Are you sure you're all right crossing the field? It can get a might bumpy."

Lily nodded. Taking a firm grip on both sides of her wedding dress, she hiked the skirt up a good six inches to keep from dragging the hem in the dirt. "Lead the way, Mister MacKinnon. I might as well see where I'm going to be living."

The humor in her words brought him joy. Not for the first time since they'd met, he said a silent prayer thanking the Lord for giving him patience. And, if he was being honest, he'd also given a word or two of thanks for Lily's train delay. Without it, they may not have ended up together.

He drew them to a stop opposite his Conestoga wagon. Not nearly as imposing as some of the others in the field, he told her, "It may not be grand, but it's much lighter in weight and should give us a definite advantage in the race."

"Very smart. Speed will make a huge difference once we break away from the pack."

Bren motioned toward the back of the wagon. "I've got a few supplies loaded already, but I didn't want to take the chance of losing anything, so most everything we'll need for the first week will be ready at the mercantile in the morning."

"Just a week's worth of supplies? Will there be somewhere along the way to get more?"

"That's another part of my plan. My uncle's friend—the one I mentioned last night—has a spread about halfway between here and where we'll be settling. His two oldest sons are going to load up building supplies, and more food stores, and deliver them to us by the end of the week. At least one of the fellows, maybe both, will stay behind to help me build a fence and start on the house."

Tentatively, it seemed, Lily lifted her hand and cradled his cheek in her warm grasp. His chest tightened from the breath he held. As he'd done to her earlier, she ran her thumb over his bottom lip.

"It would seem I've married myself a very wise husband. An adventurer who also plans ahead."

Despite his previous claims of being a patient man when it came to their marital relations, Bren couldn't deny wanting her. He needed desperately to get his longing under control. He turned his attention to the inside of the wagon.

"I've brought enough seeds and plant cuttings to give us a good start on a vegetable garden. The tools we'll need are tied down to the side of wagon. And, there's still room for our food stores and personal belongings in the back."

"I can cut down on my two traveling bags, if need be."

He gave a sound shake of his head. "That's not necessary. We'll make room for everything. We may have to sleep in bedrolls for the two nights on the trail, but once we've reached our homestead, we can move everything beneath the wagon and bed down inside." Bren paused, then offered a smile. "It won't be fancy, but I'll make sure you're comfortable."

"If I was so set on comfort, Bren, I'd have stayed in Boston."

"Come on, Missus MacKinnon, let's make a quick stop at the livery so I can check on the horses, and then we'll get that lunch I promised you."

When they arrived at the livery, the owner was busy with another customer and waved them into the massive barn. As she'd done at the field, Lily raised the hem of her skirt and followed him across the hay-strewn floor toward the far stalls.

"This place is so big," she commented as they walked. "And smelly."

He didn't bother trying to hide his chuckle, enjoying her obvious distaste for the smells most farmers took for granted. They came to a halt in front of three side-by-side stalls. "Lily, I'd like to introduce to Hank and Teddy, my Belgian draft horses." At the sound of their names, both horses moved to the door of their stalls. Bren reached into the basket nailed to the nearby wall, and withdrew some split apples, offering a half to each horse.

"Which is which?" Lily asked.

"The one with the white forelock is Hank. He can be stubborn, but he's one of the strongest animals I've ever owned. Teddy is much more agreeable, and nearly as strong."

"They're very handsome animals," she complimented.

He nudged her a few feet to the right. "And this is Duke, my gelding."

Lily scanned the horse up and down. "He's magnificent. He must be at least sixteen or seventeen hands."

Her comment caught him by surprise. "You know horses?"

"English riding horses. I took lessons for a few years but was never really interested in the whole competition part of it. I've never used a western saddle before."

"Once we're settled, I'd be happy to give you a few lessons. When the time is right, perhaps we'll even get you a horse of your own."

"I'd like that."

They stopped at the front counter and Bren paid the day's boarding fee. Nodding toward the livery owner, he told the man, "I'll be back around nine in the morning to get my animals. I'd appreciate it if you could give their shoes one final check before then."

Cyrus Michaels gave a nod. "Shouldn't be a problem. Those are three of the best cared for horses I've seen in a long time."

"Thank you," Bren acknowledged. "My uncle always told me, care for what's yours as if your life depends on it. That surely extends to these fine creatures."

Their business concluded they were on their way to lunch within minutes. Lily placed her hand in his, her slim fingers dwarfed inside his work-calloused hand. He tightened his grip slightly, reassuring himself that she was real. When she squeezed back, his heart did a fancy little jig deep within his chest.

His promise of patience was going to be the end of him, he was sure of it.

Chapter Five

Lily handed the room key to Bren and waited nervously while he unlocked the door. They'd spent the entire day together, enjoyed a delicious lunch, gone by the mercantile to confirm Bren's order, and even added on a few extra items at her suggestion. They'd talked about everything imaginable. Well, almost everything.

Tonight, they'd discuss their plans for the future, including their thoughts on family.

Given their lunch had been mid-afternoon, they'd chosen to bring some fruit and finger sandwiches back to the room with them rather than have another full meal.

"Relax," Bren whispered at her side. "I've made my promise, and I intend to stand by it until you tell me otherwise."

"I know, and that's part of what's making me so skittish," she admitted.

"How so?"

She shrugged out of her lightweight shawl and laid it aside. Turning to face her husband, she told him, "Given I—admittedly—haven't got a clue what I'm doing, I feel guilty being the one making the decision as to when... when we... consummate."

"Would you rather I demand what some men believe are their husbandly rights?"

"Well... no. Of course not."

"How about we take it as it comes? We can kiss, cuddle, and when the time is right, we'll both know it."

"I do enjoy your kisses," she told him. "And, the way you touch me... the brush of your thumb over my lips made every nerve ending in my entire being tingle."

"There, that's what I'm talking about. Slow, gentle, until you want nothing more than... well... more."

"I trust you, Bren."

At her softly spoken words, he sucked in a breath. His eyes closed, and long, dark lashes fanned over his tanned cheeks. He was, indeed, a handsome man. A kind man.

And he was hers.

"Why don't you go ahead and get out of your wedding dress," he suggested. "Behind the dressing screen, of course. Or, if you'd prefer, in the privy."

She nodded. "Let me gather my things. I could use a few moments to fresh up."

While she was collecting her gown, robe, and toiletries, Bren moved around the room, taking in the plush furnishings. "This is quite a room. One of the nicest in the hotel, I'd guess. A lot nicer than the room I'd planned to get for us."

"It was one of the few rooms they had left by the time I arrived."

"I've never seen a hotel room with its own privy before."

"I'm sure whatever room you'd have arranged would have been fine."

"I'll reimburse you the cost, of course," he told her.

"You will not," she insisted. "We're husband and wife now, we share what we have. This room is already paid for, so there's no need to quibble over the cost."

"Yes, ma'am," he responded, chuckling.

Lily clutched her bedclothes to her chest and made her way to the water closet. A moment of guilt washed over her for not being honest with Bren about her finances. She hadn't wanted the fact that she had resources to be a deciding factor in finding a husband. Now that she was married, she'd not yet found a way to bring the subject up in conversation.

By the time she washed her face, changed into her nightdress and robe, and returned to the room, Bren had turned back the covers on the bed and removed everything but his long johns and undershirt.

Her throat went dry, tight, at the sight of him. Muscles she'd only imagined beneath his white dress shirt, now shone in vivid relief beneath the thin cotton clinging to his chest. The urge to reach out and touch had her clenching her hands around the dress she'd discarded moments before.

"I thought we could get comfortable, snuggle a bit," he told her, his gaze never leaving hers, as if he was gauging her reaction.

"I... um... I still need to brush out my hair. If not, it'll be a tangled mess in the morning."

"I can do that for you," he offered, reaching for the brush on the top of the nearby dresser. "Take a seat here in front of the mirror."

Mesmerized by the look she could see in his stare, she set her discarded clothes aside and took her place on the chair. With the first stroke of the brush, her entire body trembled from head-to-toe.

Bren drew the brush through a second time, following the trail of the bristles with the sweep of his hand, setting every nerve ending in her body on full alert.

"Oh... my..." she whispered.

"Your hair is beautiful," he said softly as he continued brushing. He bent forward until he hovered close to her ear, and added, "So silky, it makes me want to run my fingers through each and every strand and draw you close to me for a kiss."

She swiveled in the chair and raised her gaze to his. "I'd like that, very much."

Bren set the brush aside. Rather than draw her to her feet, he lifted her in his arms and carried her across the room, laying her on their bed. Once she'd settled in the center of the big feather mattress, he followed her down and drew her into his arms.

"Remember. You decide when, and where."

Lily pillowed her head on his broad shoulder, and laid her hand against his chest. His muscles bunched and jumped beneath her touch, causing a heady sense of euphoria to wash over her. Through her.

Boldly, she pressed her lips to the strong column of his throat, and told him, "I choose right here, right now."

Morning came all too soon, as far as Bren was concerned. As much as had to be done this morning before the twelve-noon start of the land run, all he wanted was to make love to Lily again, and again.

No doubt, they'd both be tired and sore as the dickens for the remainder of the day. But there was no helping it. When she'd voiced her permission, her desire, it was all he could do to rein in his restraint in order to make her first time as enjoyable as possible.

Not to mention her second, and their third.

A knock sounded at the door, followed by a verbal call. "Seven o'clock warning," the anonymous voice said before moving on down the hallway.

"Oh... no..." Lily moaned at his side. "It's too early."

Bren chuckled, and pressed a chaste kiss to Lily's forehead. "Good morning, Missus MacKinnon."

"Good morning, Mister MacKinnon. As much as I'd like to roll over in this bed and have my way with you again, we've got work to do."

She sat up in the middle of the bed, and shot him a smile. "Yes, we do." Giving him a slight shove, she suggested, "Perhaps, if you can make your way out of bed, we can get this day—and our life together—started."

Bren climbed out of the bed and stood there staring down at his wife. Her eyes widened when she scanned his naked frame, her reaction only adding to his own excitement. "I'm heading to the privy. I'll be out in a couple of minutes, if you want to get your clothes ready." He grabbed the leather satchel he'd brought with him last night and made his way across the room.

By the time he came back into the bedroom, Lily was up and wrapped in her dressing gown. The new denim trousers and plaid shirt she'd bought yesterday were clutched in her grasp.

"I've got everything packed," she told him. "I won't be long getting dressed."

"Take your time," he told her. "We're not due at the livery until nine, and the mercantile by nine-thirty. We've got time to grab some breakfast in the hotel restaurant if you'd like."

"What I'd like is a cup of coffee," she told him. "The stronger, the better."

"Coffee? I pictured you being a tea drinker. Being from Boston and all."

"I do enjoy tea," she confirmed. "But nothing wakes me up like a cup of coffee with just a splash of cream."

The hotel offered what they were calling the 'runner's breakfast' consisting of a hearty plate of smoked ham, bacon, three eggs, beans, and biscuits. While he chowed down on his plate, wiping it clean, Lily only picked at hers while managing two large cups of coffee.

"Not a fan of a farmer's breakfast, I see," he said, chuckling when she pushed aside one of the fried eggs with the tines of her fork.

"I much prefer oatmeal and fruit," she told him. "Or, at least something that doesn't look as if it's dripping grease."

"It looks that way because it *is* dripping grease."

She pulled a face before pushing her plate to the side. "I'll have some fruit later, assuming there's any left when we reach the mercantile."

"I've got a half-bushel of apples on order," he told her. "I'd expected to be giving them to the horses, but you're welcome to them as well."

"I'm fine with sharing."

Bren paid the bill for their meal, and then took her hand, drawing her to her feet. "What say we get started on our grand adventure, wife?"

"Yes, let's, husband."

Lily gladly took Bren's arm as they made their way to the livery to claim the horses.

"Where's Duke's saddle?" she asked, once he led the gelding out into the paddock.

"Back at the wagon. I didn't see any sense in loading him down when he's only going to be tethered behind us."

"Will he be able to keep up?"

"It's likely I'll be having to slow him down. He was born to run. Even as fast as the wagon should go with these two Belgians pulling it, Duke will be fine."

Once all three animals were bridled, they started out, Lily leading Duke and Bren managing the two large drafts. Their next stop would be the mercantile.

The store was packed from wall-to-wall with would-be land runners, each man scouring the near-empty shelves for last minute supplies. Bren threaded his way through the throng until he'd reached the back counter, with Lily close behind and clinging tightly to his grasp.

Mister Bailey, the owner, waved them over. "Got your order right here, MacKinnon. All bagged up like you asked. Is there anything else you want to add on?"

"If you've got some extra fruit... whatever's in season... I'll take some," Bren told him.

"We've not got much fresh stuff, but my missus makes some tasty dried cranberry and nut mixes that are great for munching on when you're hungry." Bailey held up one of the paper sacks for their approval.

"We'll take a couple of bags, please," Lily confirmed. When Bren might have reached for his wallet, Lily opened her bag and withdrew her coin purse. "I'll get this," she explained. "After all, I'm the one who wanted the fruit."

Bren gave a sharp nod and then gathered up the four heaviest bags of supplies, leaving the fifth, smaller bag for her to carry.

"I could have got that, you know," he said as they were making their way to the door. "It is my responsibility."

"Do we need to review my speech on sharing again?" she teased. "Don't go getting all proud and stubborn on me. What's mine is yours. Or, more precisely, what's ours is ours."

He turned slightly so she could see his expression, and rolled his eyes. "I didn't figure you for bossy, Missus MacKinnon."

"Not bossy, just practical."

They reached the open field, and Bren's wagon, with plenty of time to get everything loaded and the horses into their tack. Then, with less than twenty minutes until the firing of the starter's pistol, Bren helped Lily up into the wagon.

"By the way, Lily, I don't believe I mentioned how fetching you look in those denim trousers. They hug all the right places."

"They do, do they?"

"Yep," he reiterated. "*All* the right places."

"I'm glad you approve. However, for the sake of our future, I'd suggest you get your thoughts off my 'places' and back on the matter at hand. If I'm reading your map correctly, we've got a lot of ground to cover before sundown."

"That we do, darling. That we do."

55

Chapter Six

The sharp echo of gunfire filled the air, setting over fifty wagons, twice as many buckboards, a few dozen carriages, and countless men and woman on horseback off on the latest land run.

Lily grabbed onto the edge of the seat as Bren set the big horses in motion. He gave the reins a sharp snap and Hank and Teddy picked up their speed. It wasn't long before they'd passed the larger wagons, and most of the buckboards, their place in the queue secured near the front.

From time-to-time, Lily glanced behind them to check on Duke, happy to see the big horse right where he was supposed to be. Holding on to keep her balance, she glanced from one side to the other. To their left, a horse stumbled, the rider hitting the dirt. Only by the grace of the Almighty was the man able to roll free of being overrun by the wagons behind him. His horse, unfortunately, did not fare as well.

Lily's stomach clenched nand roiled, the horrid sight nearly bringing her to tears. At her side, Bren tightened his grip on the reins but didn't pull the horses up.

"It's going to happen, Lily. This isn't a ride for the weak."

"I know," she responded, her voice raised to be heard over the clamor of the dozens of land runners on every side of them. "I guess I wasn't expecting to see an accident so soon."

"We'll stay to the west of the settlements claimed in the run of '89, and then stop for the night once we're halfway across the Cherokee Outlet. If we start out again early enough in the morning, we'll cross into the lands that used to belong to the Cheyenne and Arapaho by noon. That's where we'll start making our way west and cross the north branch of the Canadian River."

"You marked off a certain plot," she recalled. "F102, right?"

"Yep. There are five of the hundred-sixty acre plots that run right up to the Texas border. Plot 101 is flat, but better suited to farming. Plots 103 and 105 are hilly and have nothing more than narrow streams for water. The one I chose is flat land, backs onto an offshoot of the Washita River, and is better suited to cattle. It also has a fast running stream in the front forty."

"Perfect for watering livestock." She paused, then asked, "What about plot 104?"

"That's my backup plan if someone beats us to

my first choice."

"Well, then, I suggest we not let anyone get their first."

It was nearly twilight when they drew to halt in an area with a small brook, and trees for shelter. Three other wagons pulled in behind them. As far as Bren could tell, there were maybe four registered land runners ahead of them. With any luck, they were looking for a claim suitable for crop farming and would stay in the middle of the open lands.

Bren was leading the horses down to the water, when another man approached him, his two mules tethered behind him.

"Evening," the man said, his accent thick. "Name's Hendrickson. Olaf." He stuck out his hand. "My brother Gunter and me are looking to farm."

Bren clasped the man's hand in his. "My name's Brendan MacKinnon. My wife and I are planning to raise cattle."

Hendrickson drew to a halt, his shoulders squared. "There's been trouble between the farmers and the ranchers. Gunter and me don't want no trouble."

"Not to worry, Olaf. I got no qualms with those who want to farm. There's plenty of land to go around. The good Lord's seen to that."

"You're a Christian?" Hendrickson confirmed.

"That I am," Bren responded.

"Good. I can trust a man who respects his God."

"Do you know where you want to settle?" Bren asked.

"We're headed to F County."

"Close to the Texas border?"

"There's some great hill country right near the southern boundary with a good source of irrigation for our crops."

Bren pulled in a breath, and thought about the map he'd all but memorized over the past three days. "Plots 101 and 103 look to be good for what you need. Both have water sources and gentle slopes."

Olaf Hendrickson shot him a grin. "That's exactly what Gunter said. He's the one who knows maps. I'm the one who knows crops."

Once the animals were watered, the two men walked back to camp together. Not surprisingly, Lily was already engaged in conversation with the man Bren suspected was Gunter Hendrickson. Both brothers appeared to be in the mid-fifties.

"Bren," Lily greeted once he'd reached her side, "I see you've met Mister Hendrickson's brother. Gunter was just telling me that they're from Norway originally. Isn't that exciting, to have come all this way to take part in a land claim."

"Perhaps we'll become neighbors," Gunter suggested. "Your lovely wife tells me you're headed in the same direction as us."

"Perhaps," Bren agreed. Nodding in Lily's direction, he added, "I'm going to feed the horses, if you'd like to take out our supper."

"We'd better be getting back to our camp too," Olaf told them. "The mules will be braying for their feed if we don't tend to them soon enough."

Once he'd fed the animals, Bren started a small campfire inside the circle of rocks Lily had fashioned while he'd been off at the brook.

"I've taken out the bread and slices of dried beef," Lily told him when she'd lowered herself to sit on the blanket at his side. "I'm afraid I have no clue how to open this tin of beans."

Bren fought back the urge to laugh. He'd definitely not taken her admitted lack of cooking expertise into account when he'd chosen Lily for his wife.

"I'll do it. It takes a sharp knife and steady hand." He sat the tin can on a flat rock, and punctured the top in three spots with the tip of his hunting knife. "Once you let the pressure out, you warm them up a bit in the can before you finish opening the lid."

Lily spread out a checkered cloth across another of the larger rocks, and began setting out their food, along with a couple of spoons. "I'll take your word for it. No doubt, I'd have not thought of poking a hole in the can first and it would have exploded over the fire."

By the time they'd finished their meager meal, Lily was yawning.

"Why don't you go ahead and bed down beneath the wagon?" he offered. "I'll clean up here and join you in a few minutes."

"Um... I need to... um..."

"Ah, yes. The outdoor facilities."

"It's most uncomfortable," she admitted.

"I promise, our outhouse will be one of the first things I build."

"An outhouse," she repeated. "I suppose I can't hope for indoor plumbing any time soon."

"I've no doubt the area will build up quickly once people settle in, but not indoor privy quickly."

She gave him a broad grin. "Is it too late to turn around?"

He lifted her hand to his mouth and dusted her fingers with his lips. "Do you really want to go back, Lily?"

Her loose-hanging hair slid slowly across her

shoulders when she shook her head. "Not on your life, Brendan MacKinnon. Like you, I'm in this for the long haul. And the adventure."

By the time he made one last check on the horses, added a few scraps of wood to the campfire and made his way to bed, Lily was soundly asleep atop the pallet of blankets he'd laid out earlier.

He took his spot next to her, and pulled her into his arms, pillowing her head on his shoulder before drawing the last blanket around them.

As badly as he wanted her, he needed to remind himself they weren't alone. Closing his eyes, he willed himself to relax and accept the fact he and Lily would have all the time in the world to make love once they'd reached their new homestead.

Lily awoke the next morning exactly the way she'd fallen asleep. Alone.

Bren was in the process of dousing the last of the embers in their campfire. The horses were already hitched to the wagon. Duke was grazing on a patch of grass to the side.

She rolled out from beneath the wagon, dragging the blankets behind her. "What time is it?"

"Five-ten. I thought we'd try to get out ahead of the rest. The only other person I see milling around is Olaf, but he's not yet hooked up his team."

"I'll just make a quick run to the trees and be right back. We can have our morning meal on the road."

"I made a pot of coffee and filled the canteen before I doused the fire," Bren explained. "Between that, the leftover biscuits from the bakery in Wichita, and your fruits and nuts, we should be able to last until after we make our river crossing."

"Maybe even farther, if necessary," she suggested.

"Probably not. The river crossing isn't going to be easy. We'll likely need to have something to eat to keep up our strength."

They'd been on the road for nearly three hours when Bren pulled the wagon to a stop. "There it is," he said, nodding toward the horizon. "The northern branch of the Canadian River. If the government's maps are correct, we should be in water between two and three feet deep. I'm going to lead Duke across first and check for solid footing for the team. Once I've tied him to a tree on the other side, I'll cross back and take the wagon over. If you'd like to ride on Duke's back, that would be fine with me."

She shook her head. "No, I'll ride with you in the wagon. I don't want you to make the crossing alone."

"We'll see, once we're closer." He turned to face her directly, his warm brown gaze narrowing. "If I think it's going to be safer for you to cross on my gelding, that's the way you'll go."

Lily opened her mouth to argue, but clamped it shut when she saw the look of concern in Bren's eyes. He wasn't ordering her, as her husband, he was letting her know he was concerned for her safety, first and foremost. The realization warmed her heart.

"Fine," she said firmly, "but if it's safe enough, I'm riding with you."

Lily sat on edge of the wagon seat with her attention firmly set on her husband as he led his horse across the narrowest part of the river. The current was swift and up to Bren's waist in some parts. Wisely, he'd tied a rope to the wagon and was dragging it across with him so he'd have something to hold onto when we started back.

Twice, he'd lost his balance and slipped beneath the water and, each time, Lily had rushed to her feet, the quick motion making both Hank and Teddy snort and shift their weight.

Finally, Bren made his way onto shore, Duke climbing up the slight incline behind him. Once he'd secured Duke's reins to a sturdy tree and tied off the loose end of the rope, he began the long return trek to where Lily waited.

The moment he reached the wagon, Lily literally threw herself off the wooden bench and into his arms. "Oh, my word. You scared the daylights out of me."

He crushed his mouth to hers, the water from his wet clothes and hair soaking her clear through to the skin. Yet, it didn't matter. He was here, and he was safe.

"That was even harder than I thought it would be."

"Is there a clear path for the wagon?" Or, maybe we should wait for the others to catch up, just in case someone needs help."

"As much as I'd be happy to help someone if they needed it, I don't want to wait. The clouds are getting dark off in the distance. We need to cross before the rain starts and the river gets even deeper than it already is."

"Okay then. Let's get moving." He handed her up into the wagon but didn't climb in after her. "Bren?"

"You're riding, I'm leading and pulling in the guide rope as we go. I'll have more of a sense of the right footing if I'm walking it."

"But—"

"Don't argue with me, Lily. It's how we're

getting it done."

"At least let me handle the rope. I can draw it up as we go, and it'll be one less thing for you to do."

"Okay, but if it gets difficult, you call out and I'll take over."

They started out slowly, the first few feet going smoothly with a gradual drop. The next half dozen or so yards were far slower going, with the angle of the riverbed getting steeper by the minute.

Lily was diligently tugging on the slack rope, wrapping it around her arm as she drew it in. The wet strands of rope dug into the palms of her hands, making her wish she'd thought to put on a pair of Bren's rawhide gloves.

A sudden jolt sent the rope she'd gathered slithering through her hands, burning the surface of her skin as it unraveled. She cried out, yet the whinnies from both draft horses as they slipped and slid over the slick rocks drown out her call for help.

Bren urged the animals forward and, once the wagon had righted itself completely, the pressure lifted from the rope and she was able to regain a firm hold and continue her task.

Red stains appeared on the coiled rope and Lily realized her palms were scraped and bleeding. She brushed one and then the other against the leg of her denim trousers to wipe away the worst of the blood.

It seemed like an eternity, but they finally made it to the opposite side of the river, the two strong drafts drawing themselves, and the wagon, safely onto shore. She was about to shout out in triumph when Bren fell to his knees and bowed his head in prayer. Blinking back her tears, Lily silently gave her own thanks to the Lord for watching over them and guiding them to safety.

Chapter Seven

The rain began in earnest just minutes after they got back on the road. Lily grabbed the small tarpaulin from behind the seat and threw it over herself and Bren so they were covered from their legs to their shoulders, save for the one arm Bren kept free to hold onto the team's reins.

"Are you okay, Lily?" Bren asked, his voice muffled by the sound of the wind blowing around them.

"Other than being soaked clear through to my corselet, I'm doing fine."

Bren hadn't seen her damaged hands as yet, and she preferred to keep it that way, at least until they stopped for the night. It wouldn't do to have him insist on stopping so she could tend to her wounds.

"If we can keep moving through this muck for at least another hour or so, then we'll be less than four hours from our destination. Near as I can figure."

"How will you know where to find the markers?"

"Each plot of land will have a marker with the plot number on it at the mid point of the front forty. That's where we plant our first flag. Then, we take thirty paces in each direction north and south, to lay out our boundaries. The secret will be to find the first plot, number 104, then measure the time it takes us to get to plot 103. It should then take us the same amount of time to reach the next marker, which is the claim we want."

"Hopefully, the rain will let up by the time we stop and be sunny in the morning so it will be easier to find the right spot," Lily reasoned.

"That's what I'm praying for, Lily."

She drew his free hand from beneath the tarp and to her mouth, pressing a firm kiss on the back of his hand. "Then, I shall pray, too. Surely the Almighty will hear us, even above this wretched wind and rain."

They stopped for the night when the road was no longer discernible among the muck and mire. Thankfully, the heavy rain and tapered off to an annoying drizzle. The buckets Bren had hung on the back of the wagon were full of fresh rainwater and would provide enough for the animals, and for a pot of evening tea to go with their cold rations.

There'd be no campfire tonight, just the warmth they could find snuggled in their bedrolls beneath the wagon.

"Look," Lily said, motioning toward the trail behind them. "There's another wagon coming. I wonder if it's the Hendrickson brothers."

"I don't think so. The wagon's too large to be theirs."

The new arrivals pulled to a halt fifty feet from where Bren was tending to the horses by removing the team's tack and brushing them down.

"Evening," a man shouted. "Mind if we set up camp here with you folks?"

"Nope," Bren called back. "It's free land."

A woman poked her head out from inside the wagon. "Hi there," she said, waving her hand. "I'm Erralee. This here's my husband Micha Barrow."

Lily closed the distance between herself and the Barrow's wagon. "We're Brendan and Lily MacKinnon. Are you folks headed much farther south?"

"We're planning on setting up an orchard," Erralee told them. "Peaches and maybe some plums. We're just hoping the spot we want is still available. We'd planned on riding all night, but this rain has made everything so slippery and hard to see."

"Same with us," Lily confirmed. "But the horses needed resting, especially after slogging through this muck. And, to tell the truth, I was getting mighty uncomfortable up in that wagon for so long."

"This is a nice area here," Micha suggested. "But not part of the assigned acreage."

"Yeah," Bren agreed. "If they weren't trampled on by the land runners and buried beneath a pile of mud, these fields would be perfect for an orchard."

"How many do you think are ahead of us?" Micha asked.

"No more than three or four, I'd say," Bren explained. "With at least a couple dozen coming up on our heels."

"We made the river crossing just before the heavy rain began," Erralee told them. "The wagon after us rolled over. At that point, I think everyone else decided to camp there for the night. Or, at least until the water level went down a bit."

"Do you know which wagon went down?" Lily asked, hoping it wasn't the Hendrickson brothers.

"An older couple," Micha confirmed. "They weren't hurt, thankfully, but they lost a lot of things from their wagon. It looked like they were planning on setting up some sort of a store, rather than farming or ranching."

Erralee added, "Micha and a few of the other men were able to right the wagon before they lost everything, but then we got back on our rig and took off."

Bren grasped Lily's wrist and drew her back toward their wagon. "If you will excuse us, we're gonna grab something to eat and then hit the hay. I intend to get back on the road as soon as it's light out."

"Yeah," Micha agreed. "Us too. Have a good night."

Bren awoke just as daylight broke the horizon. The clouds were still blocking out any real hope of sun, their dark centers threatening another day of rain.

"Lily, sweetheart, wake up," he whispered, nudging his wife gently. "We need to get on the road."

She rolled onto her side and moaned. When she held up her hand to push him away, he noticed the red streaks across her palm. Drawing her other hand up to the meager light, he saw the same red streaks and a few small blisters.

What the devil?

"Go away, Cassie," she mumbled in her sleep.

"Lily Marie MacKinnon," he said more forcefully, "what the devil did you do to your hands?"

She sat up with a jolt, her sleepy gaze going directly to his.

"You're not Cassie."

"No, I'm not. Now, what happened to your

hands?"

"It's nothing," she insisted. "Just a scrape or two."

He rummaged through one of his canvas bags and dug out a pot of salve. "I'm going to go hitch the horses and fill the canteens with any collected rainwater. While I'm gone, put some of this on your hands and wrap then in something to keep the dirt out."

"I will," she told him. "Once I've done my... um... business."

"Fine," he snapped. "Be quick about it."

He regretted his sharp tone the moment the words were out. Lily's eyes filled with the threat of tears. Although, no doubt, she was too stubborn to let them fall.

"I'm sorry, Lily. I didn't mean to yell." He lifted her hand in his. "It's just I saw your hands, and... well—"

"They're fine, Bren. Nothing a bit of your salve won't fix." She paused, then added, "I'm sorry I didn't tell you about it when it happened. I didn't want you to feel like we had to stop to tend to my wounds."

"That happened when you were hauling in the rope, didn't it?"

"Yes, but—before you go blaming yourself—it

wasn't your fault. The horses slipped on the rocks and the wagon jolted. If I'd had a firmer grip on the rope, it wouldn't have slid through my hands and burned my skin. Or, better yet, the forethought to put on a pair of your work gloves."

"I should have insisted you wear them."

"Crossing that river was first and foremost on your mind, Brendan MacKinnon. Not overseeing your greenhorn of a wife."

"I happen to like watching my greenhorn of a wife," he teased.

"Go," she ordered playfully. "Hitch up Hank and Teddy, and give all three of them a handful of dried apples."

It was half past one in the afternoon when they reached the final turnoff for the stretch of claims that backed onto the Texas border. It had obviously rained even more this far south than it had during their travels.

While he held firmly to the team as they slipped and slid over the muddy, rutted path, Lily kept a close eye on the markers, watching for the first of five that should appear within the next few miles.

"There!" she called out. "I see the first one off to the right."

Bren drew the horses up. "F105." Digging into

his vest pocket, he pulled out his watch and handed it to her. "Check the time. I'll keep the wagon rolling at a steady pace so we can see how long it will take to travel between markers."

With one last glance at the unclaimed plot of land, they set out. Twenty minutes later, they pulled up to marker F104.

"This is your backup choice, right?" Lily asked.

It was all he could do to keep from jumping from the wagon and staking his claim. What if, when they reached his first choice, it was already gone? They'd have to backtrack, and run the risk of losing this claim as well.

"Can you see anyone behind us?"

Lily stood up on the wagon bed and leaned out to look around the side of the wagon. "No, it looks like we're alone, at least for a bit."

He sucked in a deep breath. "What do you think, Missus MacKinnon? Do we risk driving another hour down the road for my first choice? Or, do we take what we know is available?"

"I have faith, Bren. In you, and in God." Giving a nod of her head, she told him, "Let's go for what we want."

Bren snapped the reins and set the horses on motion, while Lily checked the watch and began counting off the minutes.

They passed the next plot, F103, the one Bren and Olaf Hendrickson had said would be a good spot for a farm, if the brothers' first choice was taken.

"Twenty minutes," Bren said beneath his breath.

The farther they traveled, the worse the roads became. Even though the rain was holding off, the ravages of the previous day were making the trip difficult.

"Three minutes," Lily exclaimed. "I don't see anyone in sight. I think we're good."

"Either that, or they've already staked their claim and they're on their way to the land office."

"Don't be silly," she admonished. "Nobody was that far ahead of us."

"Remember the Sooners from '89? They jumped the gun and crossed illegally from the south and west."

"I trust that hasn't happen this time. Slow down, we should be coming right up on it within seconds."

Bren drew the wagon to a halt. Open field lay off to the west. No red flags marking someone's right to claim. But, also, no government marker proclaiming the location. "I'm going to walk it a hundred or more feet down the road. The marker's gotta be here somewhere." When he climbed down to the ground, his feet sunk into the mud all the way past the heels of his boots. "Stay here with the wagon. If someone comes up, they may think we've already staked our claim."

"I'll lead the horses off to the side," she told him. "Hurry though, just in case we need to travel farther down the road."

Bren made his way along the rutted path, stopping every so often to glance back at where Lily was standing next to Hank's side of the wagon. Satisfied that she was safe where she was, he ventured another couple hundred feet. Surely, the thicker mud couldn't have thrown their timing off this much.

He was about to turn around and head back, when he heard a loud cry. In a panic, he took off in a run, sliding from one rut to the next as if he were on a frozen pond, rather than a muddy country road.

When he was within twenty feet of his rig, he saw Lily, flat on her backside in the mud. A full-blown laugh bubbled up from within his chest.

"Well, I'd read somewhere that people in ancient Egypt used to take mud baths for their health," he said, his words mixed with his laughter. "I ain't never seen someone try to do it here."

"Don't you be making fun of me, Brendan MacKinnon. I hurt my fanny when I landed. Who knew mud could be so hard?"

He came to a halt in front of her and offered her

his hand. "Up you go."

She tossed him a saucy grin. "Oh, by the way, when I fell, I landed on this." Lily raised up her arm, her slim fingers wrapped around a long wooden pole with a sign attached. "If you wipe the mud off, you can see it says, F102."

"I'll be... um... darned," Bren shouted. Lifting Lily off her feet, he swung her and the dirty wooden sign around in a circle. "You, my beautiful wife, are the luckiest woman I ever met. If you hadn't slipped in the mud, we'd have never known the sign was there."

Once he'd set her safely on somewhat drier ground, Bren climbed into the bed of the wagon and retrieved their claim markers. Then, leading the horses and wagon across the property line, he proudly stuck the largest of his six flags into the ground.

"I hereby claim this property as the Double L," he announced loudly.

"Double L? That's what you're calling our spread?"

He nodded, then leaned forward and pressed his lips to hers, sealing his proclamation with a kiss. "Yep, I just thought of it. Double L for Lily's Luck."

Chapter Eight

Lily helped Bren sort through the supplies in the back of the wagon. Her heart had swollen with pride when she'd watched her husband plant each one of his flags, thirty paces apart as the set of rules had instructed. Now, they were busy unloading items and placing them on a tarp beneath the wagon bed in order to make room to sleep.

Or, not sleep. The thought sent shivers of excitement down the middle of her back.

They'd been working for nearly four hours and—so far—no other travelers had ventured past.

"If you want to gather some kindling for a fire," Bren said, "I'll find us some larger stones and a few nice size pieces of dry wood so we can have a hot meal tonight."

"Once we're done eating, we could string the first row of wire," Lily suggested. "Create ourselves some temporary fencing."

"We probably should put something up, at least until Billy and Frank get here with the first of the building supplies. Their pa was going to precut our fence posts, so we'll have a permanent barrier up in no time. Once they get everything unloaded, we can take their buckboard to the designated spot where they've put up the temporary land office."

"Then, as soon as we get back, you can start on my outdoor privy."

His deep chuckle warmed her senses. "Yes, ma'am. One first class outhouse coming right up."

The sound of an approaching wagon, drew them both to the border of their property. Two overworked mules slugged through the mud, the Hendrickson's wagon limping along behind.

Bren gave a wave of his hand, and Olaf tugged on the reins.

"Good day, Bren. Missus MacKinnon." Gunter greeted. "I see you got your claim all set." Standing up in the wagon bed to stretch his back, he asked, "Has anyone else passed by? Or, is there a chance the next spot over might still be open?"

"Nobody's passed since we got here, but I can't say for certain whether or not someone may already be there," Bren confirmed.

"Well, I guess we won't know until we go look," Olaf put in. "Someone beat us to our backup site, so if we've missed out, we'll be heading east to see what's left."

"I could saddle my horse and follow you over. Help you set up your flags."

"Nah, you go ahead and stay here with the

missus. We'll be all right on our own," Gunter said.

"We'll stop and check on you when we head to the land office first thing Monday morning," Lily told them. "The good Lord willing, you'll be our neighbors."

"Amen to that," Gunter offered.

As soon as the Hendrickson's wagon was out of sight, Lily began sorting the food stuffs to organize their evening meal. Salt pork and butter beans, some cornbread—assuming she could master the recipe Bren had written out—and a pot of tea. There were four cookies left from the bakery that they'd have for a celebratory dessert after supper.

Looking out over the barren, rain-soaked land, she found it hard to fathom the difference in her circumstances in less than a few weeks. Gone were her expensive clothes and plush bed with its piles of pillows and silk coverlets. Now, her sleeping quarters consisted of a half-dozen scratchy wool blankets, two skinny pillows, and a hard, wooden floor.

Her wardrobe had become a pair of men's work pants, leather boots, and a checkered shirt. Or, if the weather permitted, a plainly trimmed dress and high button shoes. About her only concession to her old life were the expensive corselets she'd brought from home. The fancy French designs had been all the rage in Boston, and a far sight more comfortable than the traditional whalebone corsets.

"I found some decent sized stones down by the narrow creek that runs between our property and the next," Bren told her, a half-dozen rocks cradled in the bend of his arm. "If I go farther down stream, I might find some big enough to build a base around our house."

"We don't want to waste too much time building," she reminded him. "It's the sound structures that keep claim jumpers at bay."

He shot her a wicked grin. "I got a rifle and box of shells that'll do the same thing."

"You'll not be shooting anyone on our land, Brendan MacKinnon. I don't our first structure to be some poor soul's tombstone."

"I don't think I'd consider a claim jumper a 'poor soul'. However, I promise not to shoot anyone if I can help it."

At half-past seven, the sky turning dark, Lily put away the pots and pans and popped the last bite of cookie into her mouth. Bren was tending to the animals and bedding them down for the night.

With a few minutes to spare before Bren's return, Lily climbed into the wagon and stripped down to her underpinnings. A basin of water and cloth helped wash away the worst of the day's dirt.

Once she'd set everything aside, she donned her nightgown and brushed her hair. It felt good to be out of her heavier work clothes and into something as frilly as her gown.

She dug into her bag and withdrew her toiletries case. Taking out a small vial of rosewater, she dabbed behind her ears. Hopefully, her husband would appreciate the effort she'd put into looking better than a rain-soaked and bedraggled old lady.

Every muscle in his body ached, yet Bren couldn't help but feel proud of how he'd navigated his land run, claimed his plot, and put up the first signs of ownership.

Your land? His conscience prodded at him to acknowledge the fact he'd not done it alone.

"Our land," he whispered, giving the front acreage one last sweep of his gaze before heading to the wagon for a well-deserved sleep. Yes, it was *their* land. His and his new wife's homestead.

Even after spending the past three days in her company, he still couldn't believe someone as beautiful and smart as Lily O'Halloran had willingly become his bride. His partner in this new and exciting adventure.

He climbed into the back of the wagon and came

to a sudden stop. Lily was spreading out the blankets and making them a comfortable spot to sleep. Dressed in a thin, gossamer gown of pale yellow, she took his breath away.

Her long hair hung down her back, freshly brushed and free of tangles. The heavenly scent of roses consumed the entire space.

As badly as he needed it, sleep was suddenly the last thing on his mind.

"For someone who spent her day trudging through mud and her evening over a campfire, you certainly make a fetching picture, Missus MacKinnon."

She swiveled around to face him, a smile lighting her face. "And you, Mister MacKinnon, look like a man in fierce need of a good night's sleep."

"How about we compromise then? We'll get comfortable on this pile of blankets and, if I manage to stay awake long enough, we'll see about truly marking our territory."

"Hmm... I'm not sure that's truly a compromise, Bren."

He wanted to laugh but when he opened his mouth all that came out was a yawn. Sleep first. Then, making love to his wife second. Once he'd regained a good portion of his energy.

The first rays of sun were peeking through the front of the wagon. Bren shifted, drawing Lily more tightly into his arms.

Despite his desire for another hour of sleep, a foreign noise just outside the wagon had him instantly awake and on full alert. He eased Lily to the side, carefully drew his arm from beneath her body, and pushed himself to his feet.

Struggling into his trousers, he nearly lost his balance when he scrambled for the spot beneath the front seat where he kept his rifle.

The moment Bren's feet hit the dirt a man's booming voice rang out. "It's about time you got your lazy self outta bed, Bren."

Billy Waters, Pete's oldest son, stood there beside a fully-loaded buckboard while his younger brother, Frank, dozed on the front seat.

"You're early. What'd you do, start out in the middle of the night?"

"Actually, we started out yesterday," Billy explained, "but we stopped last night in one of the small towns already starting up in the middle of the run. Some smart fellow started up a saloon in the back of his wagon with two wooden tables set up for card games."

"How much did you lose?" Bren joked.

Billy threw Bren a glare. "You know better than

that, MacKinnon. I don't lose. However, there are a few would-be farmers out the money they brought to buy their seeds."

"Which is why I know better than to play cards with you."

Billy nudged his brother's foot, waking him up. "Come on you, git up. We got work to do."

Frank yawned and stretched out his lanky frame. "Dang, Billy, I was having me a nice dream."

"Yeah, well, dreaming won't get Bren's fence built," Billy shot back.

Bren set his rifle back in the wagon and made his way to the buckboard. "I truly appreciate you fellas coming out to help. Lily and me worked all afternoon and into the evening last night and managed to get some wire strung, but an honest-to-goodness fence is a permanent fixture and gives me all I need to file my claim."

"So, who is this 'Lily'?" Frank asked. "Someone you dreamed up in your imagination?"

"No, that would be me." Lily's voice carried from where she stood in the open front of their wagon. "Lily Marie O'Halloran MacKinnon."

Frank's shrill whistle rent the air. "Dang, MacKinnon, you got yourself a pretty one."

Billy was the first one to reach Lily's side, offering her his help to climb down to the ground.

The moment she put her fingers in the other man's hand, jealousy shot through Bren as quick as a flash of lightning.

"Get your grubby paws off my wife," Bren joked. Yet, deep down, he meant it.

Billy released Lily's hand and held his own up in surrender. "Just helping a lady out, Bren. No need to get riled."

"Not riled, Billy. Just cautious, given you're known to be as slick with the ladies as you are with a deck of cards."

Lily's soft snicker drew all three men's gaze. "While the three of you are posturing for head honcho, why don't I make a pot of coffee? Assuming, of course, there's any dry kindling left to restart the fire."

"I wrapped some up in the tarp last night," Bren confirmed, his sheepish grin aimed directly at his wife. "There are some bigger pieces too, so we can keep things going all day."

"There's not much for breakfast, I'm afraid," Lily admitted. "Other than some fried pork belly and beans."

"Not to worry, pretty lady," Frank told her. "We figured you'd need some fresh supplies, so we brought eggs from our chickens and a couple loaves of bread."

"That was very thoughtful," Lily replied. "A couple of eggs sounds heavenly after living off trail food for the past three days."

"We passed the stretch of government held property where the temporary land office is set up," Billy told them. "There were already two storefronts going up. And, according to one of the fellas in the card game last night, a man named Cartwright is opening a mercantile and already has stock coming in."

"I met him back in Wichita," Bren explained. "He said he was coming to the southern end of the run, so I'm glad he ended up close by. He seemed like an honest fella. He's got a wife and two or three kids, if I remember correctly."

"Wasn't there a preacher who was following the Cartwrights?" Lily commented. "He and his missus were planning to start up a church."

"Yes," Bren confirmed. "Reverend Perry Hendrian and his wife, Gracie."

"It always amazes me the way people just jump right in and build up something out of nothing," Billy said in a moment of seriousness. "When we staked our claim back in '89, there was nothing within fifty miles of where we put down our markers. Then, darned near overnight, there was a whole town sprung up. We grew so fast, they had to scramble to get us some law in place."

"Let's hope that happens here too," Bren said. "But, in the meantime, how about we get the Double L up to snuff?"

"The Double L?" Frank repeated.

"Yep, named it after my beautiful wife and her uncanny ability for finding things, even when they're buried in mud."

Chapter Nine

Lily sorted through the dirty clothes they'd accumulated over the past few days. Before Bren and Billy left to survey the back end of the property, Bren had brought her buckets of water for the huge washtub that had taken up one entire corner of their wagon.

"Let me know when the water's hot, Missus," Frank reminded her. "I'll carry the buckets to the tub for you."

"Thank you, Frank. And, please, call me Lily. Bren and I appreciate you and your brother coming to help us get set up."

"Pa insisted, although we were happy enough to get out of the fields for a week or so anyway."

"What crops do you farm?" she asked.

"Mostly corn and beans, but we got a few smaller fields planted as well. Plus, we keep the chickens for eggs, and a half dozen cows for milk and butchering."

"I'm hoping we can have a decent sized garden here, in addition to our cattle of course."

Frank returned to his assigned job of digging the holes for the fence posts, stopping every-so-often to wipe sweat from his blond brows. Not nearly as tall as either Bren or the older Billy, Frank was stocky and strong. Lily marveled at the way the young man was able to carry two of the heavy fence posts on each shoulder and set them out at the measured distance.

While she waited for the water to heat, she surveyed the items set out beside the washtub. There was a bag of soap shavings and a strange looking contraption that Bren said was the scrub board. She sucked in a breath and wished she'd paid more attention when Emmaline had offered to teach her some domestic chores.

How difficult could it be? After all, it was just soap and water.

Frank sidled up to where she was eyeing the washing supplies, a chuckle escaping as he walked. "I take it you've never washed clothes in a tub before."

"Is it that obvious?" she asked, echoing his laugh.

"Don't worry none, I'll walk you through it. As the youngest, I'm often stuck with scrubbing the dirty clothes. I've become an expert at it, pretty much."

"Well then, I guess my lesson is in good hands."

By the time Bren and Billy returned from the back forty, Lily had finished washing their clothes and hung everything on a line Frank strung from the wagon to a nearby tree. A sense of accomplishment filled her chest. While not the most daunting of tasks, of course, at least she was contributing and not just sitting there like a simpering, pampered princess.

"Is that coffee I smell?" Billy asked as he dismounted. "Hmm... chicory, right?"

"Yep," Bren confirmed. "Some of my late uncle's special blend. I brought the last two tins with me."

"I made sandwiches," Lily told them. "They're wrapped up in the checkered cloth over by the fire."

"Great," Billy acknowledged, setting a straight course for the coffee pot. "I'm as hungry as a spring bear."

"How does the rest of the land look?" Lily asked. "Is it as flat as you'd hoped?"

Bren took a seat on a pile of wooden planks and unwrapped his sandwich. "There's some natural separation between our place and the other parcels on both sides. There are trees and a free-running stream between us and the plot to the north, and a nice little pond over toward the south property line."

"Yeah," Billy agreed. "That pond will be a great place to take a dip after a day out in the hot sun."

"I could definitely use a swim," Frank admitted. "Putting up fencing is hard work."

"Well, now that the posts are in," Bren explained, "the three of us should be able to get the boards up in no time. Once we've secured the front of the property, we can start on the foundation for the house."

"When are you two heading to the land office?" Billy asked.

"Hopefully, first thing Monday morning," Lily confirmed. "I've got a supply list started, so if you fellows think of anything, let me know and I'll add it on."

"Billy and me will keep working on the house while you're gone. Or, if you'd rather, we can start putting in the fence posts down one side of the property line."

"What about the back forty?" Lily asked. "Did you get a look at where we come up to the Texas border?"

"There's a fence up on the Texas side. A big one," Bren confirmed. "I've a mind to find out who owns that nice piece of property and see if I can cut a deal with him to run my fencing up to where his starts in exchange for helping him with any necessary repairs some time in the future."

"If they're cattlemen, like you intend to be,"

Frank pointed out. "They'll likely welcome the help, especially if it keeps your herds from mixing."

Lily listened intently as the three men plotted out their work plans, sorting out who would do what, and which of the buildings could wait. A faint flush warmed her cheeks when Bren insisted the outhouse be one of the first permanent structures.

Lily was up bright and early on Monday morning. Bren had slipped out of the wagon only moments before. Frank and Billy were still asleep in the huge tent they'd set up when they first arrived.

Today was the day they'd make the formal claim for their homestead. They'd also be getting their first look at the progress of the merchants who were setting up a nearby town. The realization that she was part of creating an entire new community in this empty countryside was far grander than any adventure she'd ever imagined. If her sisters and parents could see her now, Lily felt certain they'd be proud of what she'd accomplished.

Or, at least, she hoped they would.

"Are you ready to go, Lily?" Bren asked once they'd finished their breakfast. "Billy and Frank have their buckboard unloaded so we can take it to town and load it up again."

Lily tucked her hand into Bren's and followed

him forward. When his fingers tightened slightly around hers, she squeezed back. It wasn't much in the way of intimacy, but all they had at the moment what with Frank and Billy sleeping only a few dozen feet from their wagon.

She spared a moment's thought for Bren's sweet goodnight kisses. It felt right, as if this was exactly where she was supposed to be, and who she was supposed to be with. No matter how unconventionally their marriage had begun.

The ride to the land office—known simply as Cheyenne Claim Depot—took a little less than hour and that included a brief stop by the plot next to theirs to assure themselves the Hendrickson brothers would be their neighbors.

All seemed right with the world.

Which usually meant, something was about to go horribly wrong.

Bren helped her down from the wagon and led the way into the hastily constructed building. A single clerk sat behind a high counter, a half dozen ledgers spread out in front of him. Two other customers stood off to the side waiting their turn, while an elderly couple were front and center staking their claim.

Lily could tell Bren was nervous. His gaze darted around the room, from one man to another. She recognized one of the men from Missus Miller's mixer. The fellow had ended up marrying the schoolmarm in a ceremony before the judge.

"Next," the clerk shouted.

The elderly couple made their way out of the office, a piece of paper clutched tightly in the man's grasp, while the next fellow in line approached the counter.

It seemed to be taking forever, but it was finally their turn.

"I'm here to stake my claim," Bren said, his voice filled with confidence. "Here's the government marker," he added, holding up the wooden sign, minus the heavy stake.

"F county, Plot 102," the clerk mumbled, reaching for the book allotted to that section of the run. Once he'd flipped open the page, he raised his head and met both hers and Bren's gaze head on. "That plot's already been claimed."

At her side, Bren's entire body tensed. His hand closed tightly around hers, almost to the point of hurting.

"It can't be," Bren argued. "There were no flags put up. No structures. And," he added for good measure, "I brought in the government marker. Which was the first rule of the land run."

The man had the good sense to look

embarrassed. "I don't know what to tell you… um… but it's right here in black and white." He spun the ledger around so they could read the entry.

"Plot F102, Cyrus Wilson, April 18, 1892," Lily read aloud. Shifting her gaze from the page to the man's face, she told him, "That can't be right because the run didn't start until the nineteenth. This Mister Wilson, whomever he is, had no right to stake a claim before the race even started."

The man held up his hands. "I'm not doubting you're correct. However, this claim was signed off by my boss. I do know that Mister and Missus Wilson also have a piece of the town plot. They bought into that when the land association split up eighty acres for development. Each person wanting to start a business paid a hundred dollars for their section of the plot along what's gonna be the main street. They also get a section off at the end of the main road to build themselves a house in town."

"So, how did he also end up with a claim on my land?" Bren asked heatedly. "Wasn't it supposed to be one plot per family?"

"The town plots are separate from the homesteading plots. Maybe he and his missus plan to build their home outside of town."

"The rules also state that, not only are flags required to be set up, but at least one permanent structure has to be installed before a claim can be made," Lily pointed out. "We're the only ones who've done any of that."

"You got every right to protest," the clerk reminded them. "My boss will be back on Wednesday. You can take it up with him then. Or, if you've a mind, you can track down Mister Wilson and see if he might want to sell the plot to you."

"Sell it?" Bren roared. "How can he sell me something that's rightfully mine?"

Before her husband's anger got the better of him, Lily asked, "Where might we find this Mister Wilson?"

"He's setting up his saloon down the road a few doors past the mercantile and at the opposite end of where they're building the church."

"Fine, thank you. We'll be back shortly."

Bren reached out and snatched the wooden marker from the top of the counter, and added, "Count on it," before heading for the door.

Chapter Ten

Bren tugged on Lily's hand and led her to the buckboard. His entire plan… his life… just went down the drain on what appeared to be a false claim. He'd get this straightened out. Right here and now.

"Bren," Lily said softly, her gentle use of his name intended—no doubt—to take the edge off his anger.

As much as he loved the dulcet tone of her voice, he wasn't about to cool off. Not yet anyway. "We'll get to the bottom of this, Lily. I intend to let that scoundrel Wilson know he can't cheat his way into my claim."

"However he came about the claim, it's been registered so it's official. Our only recourse may be to buy it from him, if he's willing."

Bren thought briefly of the money he had left in his pocket, and the extra he'd squirreled away in a hiding spot inside the wagon. He had enough for more supplies and for his first dozen head of cattle but—until there was a bank set up in town—he couldn't get to the money he'd left behind for safe keeping. Having to purchase land that should rightfully be his would cripple him.

"Let's see if we can reason with the man first. Then, we'll worry about having to shell out money we don't have."

"I... um—"

"Don't you worry none, darling. I'll make sure we don't lose our claim."

The storefront designated as *Sneaky Sal's* was nearly complete, the swinging doors in the process of being installed.

"This is it?" Lily asked when Bren pulled the horses to a halt.

"Yes, I guess it is. And no place for a lady. So, you'll stay out here and wait while I go put the fear of my rifle into this fellow."

Lily pushed herself to her feet in the bed of the wagon. The force with which she stood sent him backpedaling a few steps.

"I'll do no such thing, Brendan MacKinnon. If you're going to bargain with the man, I want to be there to make sure you don't do anything rash."

"Rash? Like what?"

"Like try to shove your rifle down the man's throat."

Realizing she wasn't going to back down, Bren lifted Lily to the ground. "Fine. Let's go see what this fellow has to say for himself."

The interior of the saloon was taking shape even

faster than the exterior. The bar was nearly built, the shelving to hold the bottles of hooch already up and waiting. A man and a woman were working to set up tables in the middle of the open, wood plank floor.

"Excuse me," Bren called out. "I'm looking for a Cyrus Wilson."

A stocky man with a grizzled beard turned around. "I'm Cyrus Wilson. What can I do for you?"

"Well, for starters, you can release the claim you filed on my land."

"Your land?" Wilson repeated. "What land would that be, fella?"

The woman turned to face them as well, her faded gray gaze raking both him and Lily from head to toe. "You must be talking about that parcel outside of town."

"Yes," Bren confirmed. "The one that hasn't been properly claimed with flags and buildings. At least not until I got there."

"We bought that claim fair and square from the land office. It's not our fault they didn't take it off the list before the run started," Mister Wilson told them.

"You can't buy land that's been designated as part of the land run," Lily pointed out. "It's right there in the rules."

"What can we say?" Missus Wilson put in. "The

land office fella was more than happy to take our hundred dollars and write our names down in his book."

Bren sucked in a breath, and asked, "Are you willing to sell it? Or, do you plan to build outside of town?"

"Naw, we're staying close to our business," Cyrus confirmed. "Building ourselves a little cabin on the edge of town. As for selling, that's up to my missus. She's the one who talked the land fellow into selling it to us."

Missus Wilson shot Bren a crooked smile. "I can be very persuasive."

"What do you want for the property?" Lily asked.

"Five hundred ought to do it," the woman said.

"Five hundred?" Bren shouted. "That's more then three times what you paid for it. Illegally, at that."

Lily's grip tightened against his.

"We'll give you two-fifty, right now," Lily said firmly. "And you'll sign off on the deed transferring the property over to us."

"Lily?" Bren whispered. Leaning close, he told her, "I don't have that kind of money with me."

"Well?" Lily prompted, meeting the older woman's stare. "Do we have a deal?"

"We gotta think on it," Cyrus offered. "Come back later."

Bren took a step closer to the bar. "Or, we could just contact the marshal's office in Oklahoma City and make them aware of the crooked deal you cut with the state's local land official. Maybe get us a lawyer and take you before a judge."

"Yeah, okay. We got a deal. Why not?" Missus Wilson agreed. "That gets us back the money we paid for both claims, with fifty bucks to spare." The woman held out her hand. "Fork it over."

Much to his surprise, Lily reached into her purse and withdrew a leather wallet. Carefully, she counted out the tens and twenties. "There. Two-fifty." When she laid the money on the bar, Cyrus reached for it. Lily clamped her hand over the cash, and proclaimed, "Not so fast. Deed first, money later. Now, start writing."

Mister Wilson lifted a wooden box from behind the bar and flipped open the lid, withdrawing the formal paperwork for plot F102. On the back of the deed, he wrote down the date of sale and signed it.

"Nice doing business with you," the man sneered. "I hope to see you in my establishment when I'm open for customers."

Bren shook his head. "There's not a chance that's going to happen."

Deed in hand, Bren put his arm around Lily's shoulders and led them out through the front door, the Wilsons' laughter ringing in his ears.

Once they're reached the sidewalk, he spun Lily around until their gazes met.

"What the devil, Lily? Where'd you get that money?"

"What do you mean? It's my money. I brought it with me from Boston."

"Really? Just what other important things are you hiding?" When she didn't answer, he snapped, "I won't abide by my woman keeping secrets from me."

It was obvious Bren was angry. Yet, Lily had no intention of letting him bully her. His *woman*, was it? Not his wife. The term made her sound like a harlot.

"I'll have you know, Brendan MacKinnon, that I don't abide by being spoken to with disrespect. I am not your 'woman', I am your wife. For better or worse."

"We need to talk about this, in detail," he insisted. "I'll not have you making deals and paying for things that are my responsibility."

She planted her balled-up fists firmly on her

hips and glared at him. "There is no single responsibility in a partnership, Bren. Isn't that what marriage is supposed to be… a partnership."

Rather than respond to her question, he asked, "Why didn't you tell me you were carrying all that money?"

She released a sigh, wishing she'd found the time to bring up finances long before now. Long before it came as a shock to her husband.

"I didn't mention it at first because I didn't want a prospective husband to see me only as a woman with means, rather than a possible wife." Meeting his gaze, she admitted, "I was worried people would think I was buying myself a husband."

"Once we were married, you should have said something."

"You're right, I should have, but I never found the right time."

His dark gaze narrowed with suspicion. "How hard would have been to say, 'oh, by the way, husband, I have a few hundred dollars in my purse'? Or, some such thing."

Oh, dear. If she spoke up now, she had no doubt things would get even more complicated. So, instead, she suggested, "How about we discuss the issue of money later this evening? Right now, we need to make our way back to the land office and finalize our claim. And, then, pick up some supplies."

"Okay, but don't think this whole talk about what you're hiding from me is over? I won't abide by secrets in this marriage."

"Well then, husband, you're in luck because neither will I."

Once their claim was properly filed and their errands complete, Lily climbed onto the seat of the buckboard and waited for Bren to pay the merchant for the lumber and paint.

No doubt the ride back to the site would be tense. Bren's anger still simmered at the surface. Other than to help her in and out of the wagon, he barely touched her. When she'd reached for his hand at the last stop, he'd shoved his fist into the pocket of his trousers rather than clasp her fingers in his.

His slight had hurt. Obviously, Bren was a proud man. One who didn't believe in living off a woman. Well, she had news for him. If there's was to be a true partnership, he'd have to accept her help from time-to-time.

When they arrived at their property, Lily was delighted to see the Waters brothers had constructed her coveted outhouse. They'd even adorned the doorway with a carving of Bren's design for the Double L brand.

"Took you long enough," Billy called out as Bren pulled the wagon into the yard.

"There was a problem," Bren grumbled. "Some weasel had paid off the land officer and laid claim to my property."

"What happened?" Frank asked. "Did you get it straightened out? Or, did we just do two days work for someone else?"

"We got it sorted," Bren growled. "Had to buy the property back, but it's all good now."

"You could have filed a dispute," Billy suggested. "Taken it to the law."

Bren shook his head. "That's take too long and would halt us building anything. I intend to get my homestead up and running before summer."

'*My homestead*'. Bren's words rang like a church bell in Lily's head. Not, 'our homestead', but just his.

"I'll get supper started," she told them. "We picked up a dressed chicken and a fifty pound sack of potatoes, along with fresh bread and a spice cake."

"Sounds good to me," Frank responded. "I'm gonna slip down to the pond for a quick dip. That sun was so hot today, it almost makes me miss the rain."

"Not me," Bren responded. "The faster we get

this work done, the better. I'm planning to attend my first cattle auction in June, so the fencing needs to be up before then."

"What have they got built in town?" Billy asked, his question aimed at both Bren and her.

"The saloon is almost done," Lily told him. "Although, I wouldn't trust the owners. There's a mercantile, but only about half of his stock has arrived. A butcher and poultry shop. A café, although at the moment the woman's main business appears to be selling her baking."

"There's a jail going up," Bren added. "And the livery is almost complete, other than his forging equipment is still on the way."

"Have they named the town yet?" Frank asked as he came out of the tent with a flannel shirt and clean pair of denim trousers thrown over his shoulder.

"Talk is they're going to name it Cheyenne. That's what they're calling the land office now, so it'll likely stick," Bren told them.

"I think it's very nice of them to name the town after one of the tribes who used to occupy this land," Lily commented.

While Lily attempted to cook her first chicken, and Frank went to clean up in the pond, Bren and Billy worked on the closest stretch of fencing. This is how it should be, Lily realized. A team working to achieve a goal. Perhaps she should take the proverbial bull by the horns and tell her husband exactly what she envisioned for their life together.

Chapter Eleven

Just after dusk, Billy and Frank set out for town in search of a couple of drinks and a game of cards, leaving her and Bren alone for the first time since the brothers arrived.

"I need to apologize," Bren said.

When he came to stand behind her and wrap his arms around her middle, Lily sank into his embrace.

"There's no apology necessary, Bren. I should have been more forthcoming with my circumstances."

"Still, there was no reason for me being so ornery over you paying to secure our land."

There it was—what she'd prayed for—his acknowledgement that this was *their* land. She stroked her fingertips across the back of his arm and leaned more fully into his hold. "I can understand your feelings. You wouldn't be the first man to be upset or embarrassed by a woman paying for something."

"I shouldn't have let my male pride get in the way of what had to be done."

She drew a breath, and told him, "There's nothing wrong with wanting to be the provider,

Bren. It's a most noble pursuit. However, times are changing. Women have more power than ever. We only recently earned the right to own property. I hold out hope some day that we'll be allowed the right to vote." Pausing to gather her thoughts, she added, "*That* is when this country will see real progress."

Bren leaned forward and pressed a gentle kiss to the side of her throat. "I have no doubt in my mind, my beautiful wife, that you'd turn the country on it's ear if you were ever allowed to make its political decisions."

"Do you know why I never married? Can you even image what it's like to be paraded before a string of acceptable suitors in hopes of making a business match, rather than a love match?"

"I truly have no idea why some man wouldn't want to scoop you up, Lily. And, to tell the truth, I think we were both a bit 'paraded' at Missus Miller's marriage mart."

"Yes, I suppose we were. However, I was far more amenable to being able to choose who I'd speak to, rather than have to feign courtesy to the most detestable men."

"Oh, yeah," he responded, chuckling. "Being forced to be nice to all those rich businessmen and solicitors must have been a horrible fate."

"It was. Truly."

"Tell me, Lily MacKinnon, why have you never married? Before me, that is."

"Well, according to my mother... I'm opinionated, out-spoken, brash to the point of being brutally honest and rude, and totally lacking in the finer graces. Despite the money they spent sending me to finishing school."

"I love... um... like your honesty. You don't play games like some other women. However, I think there's more to your decision to not marry than just your unabashed honesty."

I was waiting for you. The thought came to her in a flash and she wished she had the nerve to say it out loud. Instead, she told him, "I wasn't interested in what those men had to offer as far as prestige or money. I wanted a love match."

Bren's arms tightened around her and he drew a breath. "Instead, you got me."

"And I couldn't be happier," she admitted. "Especially now that you've built me this absolutely beautiful outhouse."

His laughter tickled her senses. "Well, truthfully, it was Frank and Billy that built it. I just insisted on it."

"As long as we're having this discussion, perhaps we should get everything out in the open."

"Such as?"

"First off, my idea of what our partnership should be all about."

Bren nuzzled behind her ear, and whispered, "I'm listening."

"We each bring different strengths to this arrangement. Well, to be truthful, you bring far more to it than I do. What you offer in ambition, knowledge, brut strength, and patience—especially with me—I can match in other ways. Ways that will benefit our partnership." She closed her eyes, drew a deeper breath, and told him, "For instance... money. It takes a lot to start up a new homestead, and I'm willing to pay my fair share. More than my fair share, actually."

Turning her in his arms until they were toe-to-toe, breath-to-breath, he asked, "Just how much more money did you bring with you, other than the two-fifty you gave the Wilsons?"

"Oh, I've only about six-hundred dollars left, but—"

"Six hundred? Do you realize how many more head of cattle we could buy with that? Or, even use it to build a bigger house."

She raised her chin, locking gazes with his warm brown eyes. "There's more."

"More what?"

"Money, silly. I've got a trust fund. Money left to me by my late grandparents on my mother's side."

"Jeez, Lily." Shaking his head, he asked, "Do I even want to know how much?"

She shrugged, the lift and fall of her shoulders causing Bren's hands to slide up and down her arms. "Only if it matters to you. Truthfully, I rarely give the money a second thought."

"Said like someone who's never had to worry about drought, or floods, or whether or not they can feed their family."

She couldn't tell if his comment was meant in jest, or was he truly upset at her revelation. "My circumstances shouldn't matter, Brendan MacKinnon. I'd have entered into this marriage, this adventure, whether either of us had money or not."

He pulled her forward and pillowed her head on his shoulder. Sighing deeply, he told her, "I hope you still feel that way six months or a year from now, when the work gets harder, the weather more challenging, and you still don't have your indoor privy."

"Don't be ridiculous, Bren. I will have my indoor privy far sooner than that. Even if I have to build it myself."

The tension drained from his big body and he admitted, "That's something I'd like to see.

Although, perhaps, we should begin with those cooking lessons I've been promising you."

Lily stepped back and took his hand in hers, tugging gently to set them in motion. Leading the way to the wagon, she told him, "Or, perhaps, there are other—more important—things you can teach me. At least for tonight while we're alone."

When Bren awoke the next morning, Lily was already up and setting the campfire for their breakfast and the first—of many—pots of coffee. At some point during the night, the brothers had returned. Their horses were tethered to a stake in the grassy knoll beside Duke, with Hank and Teddy not far away.

He climbed down from the wagon, tucking his shirt into his trousers as he made his way across the distance between himself and his wife. "Good morning, Missus MacKinnon," he said, pressing a kiss to her cheek. "Did you sleep well?"

"Eventually," she teased. "How about you?"

"Like a lamb. Eventually."

"You two doin' some sort of lovey-dovey thing over there?" Frank joked as he emerged from the tent. "I don't want to be seeing no smoochin' before I've even had my coffee."

"Mind your own beeswax," Bren warned. "I was just giving my wife a morning peck on the cheek."

"What's the plan for today?" Frank asked. "Where are we starting at first?"

"I want to get a firm foundation down for the house," Bren explained. "I was going to take your buckboard and follow the creek to where it flows into the larger body of water. I'm hoping to find enough large stones to mud over the wooden base."

"Morning," Billy grumbled as he made his way from the tent to the campfire. "A stone base will look mighty nice. How about me and Frank get started on digging the root cellar and lining the walls with boards while you're off hunting rocks?"

Lily poured them each a cup of coffee from the enamel pot before joining in the conversation. "I was thinking I'd plot out our garden. Maybe sketch out a pattern so we know where to put each plant."

"Have you given more thought to a chicken coop?" Frank's question aimed at them both, he added, "There's nothing beats fresh laid eggs."

"You've talked me into it," Bren agreed. "I'd not planned on chickens, but it'll be cheaper than buying them in town."

By eight that morning, everyone had taken to their tasks. Bren gave a slight squeeze to Lily's hand before climbing up on the seat of the buckboard. "I'll be back by lunch. With any luck, I'll have a wagon full of smooth stones to add to our foundation."

"I've no doubt, Bren, you'll find exactly what we need."

It was half-past twelve when Bren pulled the horses up close to where the main house would be built.

"It looks like you found exactly what you were looking for, and then some," Billy commented, his attention given to the wagon-load of small to medium size stones. "We got the cellar dug, and Frank's just finishing lining it with boards."

"He's leaving space between them right, so the damp earth will keep the cellar cool?"

"Yep, he knows what he's doing... for a kid."

Bren jumped down from the wagon and gave Billy a sound clap on the shoulder. "You only call him a 'kid' because you're pushing being an old man. Don't you think it's about time you get yourself a woman and settle down, like me."

"Nope. Not interested," Billy proclaimed. "I'm perfectly fine with the ladies at the Lazy Dog back home."

"Whatever you say, Billy. You'll change your mind one day, though. Most likely when you least expect it." Glancing around the property, Bren asked, "Where's Lily?"

"The last I saw of her she was walking off the area she's got planned for her garden." Giving a jerk of his head, Billy motioned toward the open field left of the foundation. "Somewhere that way."

"Thanks. I'll go find her so we can get started with lunch."

Bren was about to walk away, when Billy chuckled. "She doesn't know how to cook, does she?"

"Not yet," Bren admitted. "But she's learning."

"Never met myself a woman who didn't know how to cook."

"That's because you never met a gently raised lady who never had to learn how to cook," Bren pointed out. "Like you said, you're more the saloon girl type."

Lily stood back and marveled at the sight before her. This had been their most productive day so far. Hers and Bren's home now had a foundation, a root cellar, and the skeleton of a two-storey house.

She'd put in poles and run string to mark the boundaries of her garden. And now, while their supper was cooking over the campfire, the three men were digging up the earth and turning it over so they could put out the seeds and starter plants Bren had brought from his Kansas home.

Even a light drizzle of rain in the mid afternoon hadn't dampened their spirits.

"You fellows get washed up," she called out. "Supper's going to be done in less than a half hour."

"We'll be there in a few minutes," Bren hollered back. "We've got another five feet to turn over before we call it quits."

Yes, it was all coming together. In less than a month's time, she'd gone from a pampered city dweller, to a frontier wife. Her grand adventure had turned out to be even more exciting—and definitely more challenging—than she'd originally expected.

Chapter Twelve

Double L Ranch
Wednesday, May 18, 1892

Lily set aside the watering can, took one last quick perusal of her fledgling garden, and then made her way to the front porch. The tea she'd set earlier should be perfectly steeped. The biscuits Bren taught her to make, and the jam she'd bought in town, awaited her on the table next to her rocking chair.

A light flush warmed her cheeks when she thought back about the baking lesson her husband had given her, and of how something as simple as mixing up a pan of biscuits could turn into something far more exciting.

The sensual memory drew her smile.

Bren had gone into town on some mysterious mission earlier that morning. Ever since Billy and Frank had left two days earlier, Bren was itching to find himself a ranch hand he could trust. Preferably someone with experience handling cattle.

She was about to refill her tea cup when the sound of an approaching visitor pulled her gaze.

"What in heaven's name, Brendon MacKinnon," she said, as she descended the stairs and crossed the yard. "What is all of this?"

His broad grin set her heart racing.

"It's for you," he told her. "Your own method of getting around. Although, you will need to use either Hank or Teddy in the harness. Duke definitely doesn't care for pulling a rig of any kind." As if he understood and agreed, the big gelding gave a snort of displeasure at having been put upon as a draft horse.

Lily made her way around the two-seater buggy with the fancy fringed roof. "But why?"

"I figure there may be times when I'm busy out in the pasture, and you might want to go into town on your own. Even though we've stripped down the Conestoga to little more than a buckboard, it's still a lot to handle."

"I wasn't expecting—"

Bren hopped down from the bed of the buggy and drew her into his arms. "Happy Anniversary, Lily."

"Anniversary?" she squeaked.

"Yes, we've officially been married one month today," he reminded her.

"Oh... right." She swallowed, a slight quiver in her voice. "I didn't get you anything."

"That's okay," he whispered, his lips pressed to her temple. "You've given much more than you know just by being my wife. Plus, I got myself something, too."

"Really?" Raising her gaze to meet his, she added, "Please tell me it's not another chicken. Eight is enough for a start."

"Nope. I found myself a foreman. Someone who knows this land even better than we do."

"That's wonderful. When does he start?"

"He'll not begin working until just before we go to the cattle auction. There's nothing for him to do at the moment."

"What about helping you build the bunk house? And, what's his name? Where is he from?" Her questions came so rapid-fire she nearly lost her breath.

Her excitement drew Bren's chuckle. "He's got a place in town, so no need for a bunkhouse until we have to hire more men. As for his name, it's Jerry Blackcrow. He's half Cheyenne, and half white on his mama's side. He grew up in these parts. When the Cheyenne and Arapaho were relocated, he was allowed to stay because of his mixed heritage and because he has a white wife, and they have an infant son."

"So, they have their own homestead?"

"No, not exactly. They were able to buy into the town plot for the wife's business. She's a seamstress. They have living quarters above her storefront."

"I look forward to meeting them."

"I haven't met the wife yet, but he seems like a descent fellow. He definitely knows his way around animals."

"That's exactly what you need then, isn't it?"

"For the time being, it'll be perfect. At least until we expand." He paused, catching her attention. "Oh, I nearly forgot, you got a letter. Mister Cartwright was holding it at the mercantile."

"Mister Cartwright?"

"Yep, his store has been designated as the drop off for the mail coming in from outside the territory." Bren released the light hold he'd taken on her shoulders, and dug into his back pocket, pulling out a crumpled white envelope. "He's even built a big box with separate slots for each of the F County plots."

"It's from my parents," she said, scanning the return address on her mother's fancy stationery. "I'm so happy they got the telegram I sent just before we left Wichita."

"I wonder what would have happened if we'd not secured our spot after you'd already sent them the particulars?"

"I'm not sure," she admitted. "Although, I had absolutely no doubt in your ability to succeed."

"Your faith in me is humbling, Lily. It's what gives me strength when I'm weary."

"Speaking of faith, how is the church coming along?"

"It's done, other than to paint the inside. According to Reverend Hendrian, services are scheduled for this coming Sunday at ten."

"Wonderful," Lily exclaimed. "We can make the drive in my brand new buggy." Tugging on his hand, she told him, "Come and have a cup of tea. Let's see what my mother has to say in her letter."

Lily took her seat in her favored rocking chair, while Bren settled himself on the porch railing and leaned against the nearest post.

"I hope your parents aren't sending someone to cart you home," he teased.

"It's not likely I'd go without a darned good fight. After all, I am an adult, and legally married. They can't just up and take me. Besides, I'm sure my parents are overjoyed that I've made my own life."

She tore into the envelope and withdrew four sheets of paper, one from each member of her family. Giving her husband a half-smirk, half-smile, she chose the first missive on the top of the pile. Her mother's beautiful script nearly jumped off the page.

Reading the letter aloud, she began, '*Lily, dearest. To quote you... Are you out of your mind? A farm wife on barren land?*' Lily raised her gaze to Bren's. His jaw twitched with the effort of holding in his laugh. She continued. '*Come home this instant. You weren't made for this type of hard work and challenge. You're a lady, not some dirt farmer.*'

"Let me guess. She's not happy with your situation," Bren put in when she'd stopped to draw a breath.

"My mother, for all her complaining about my unabashed honestly, is just the same. However, she does it in an entitled, snobbish way." Meeting his broad grin, she told him, "I'm sorry if her words are offensive. She has no idea what a wonderful man you are, and what a perfect life we're building together."

"Wonderful man, am I?" His grin widened, sending a twinkle to his eyes.

Lily scanned the rest of her mother's letter quickly. "She goes on to tell me about what I'm missing out on in Boston. And, she goes on to assure me that Mister Hillebrand, the man she'd hoped I'd marry, has found himself another would-be wife." Biting her lip to hold in her own laugh, she admitted, "I feel sorry for the unknown woman."

"While you finish your letters, dearest, I'm going

to go unhitch my cranky horse and put him out to graze. I also have a few supplies to unload from the back of the buggy. You can give me the overall summary of their well wishes later."

Dearest. He'd called her 'dearest'. Lily's pulse fluttered. Given how strong her own feelings had become for Brendan MacKinnon, Lily's heart filled with the notion that perhaps—with time—he'd come to love her as surely as if theirs had been a love match from the very beginning.

The last dregs of her tea swirling in the bottom of the cup, Lily moved on to her father's short, two-paragraph, note. As she'd assumed he would, her father wished her well, gave her a handful of fatherly warnings about men, and asked for a return letter to recount her progress on their new home.

She moved to the next letter, written in her youngest sister Becca's flowery scrawl. *'Darling sister, we were so surprised to hear your news. Marriage to a complete stranger. How horrid that must be to have not been properly courted. I, myself, have become engaged to a wonderful young man, Mister Randolph Hastings, of the Cambridge Hastings. He's to be a doctor one day, as soon as he finishes medical college. Our wedding is set for next spring, right after my nineteenth birthday. He is most handsome, although a little short for my taste.*

However, his family has money and standing, so I will have a fine future, I am sure.'

What had happened to the match with William Hildebrand? Leave it to Becca to gloss over the important stuff and only talk about herself in the most glowing terms.

Lily moved on to the final letter from her sweet Cassie. No doubt, Cassie will be more forthcoming with all the best gossip.

'Lily Marie, you sneaky, sneaky girl. Shame on you for not telling us you were not only going west but planning to marry as well. I truly hope this Mister MacKinnon is handsome and to your liking. As for me, I am engaged to William Hildebrand. Can you believe it? He chose me, rather than Becca. Rupert wasn't too broken up about it, as I believe he has his sights set on a widow whose husband left her with tons of money.'

How wonderful for Cassie. Lily glanced at her empty tea cup, wishing there were more in the pot, for Cassie's letter filled both sides of the linen stationery.

'Yesterday was Emmaline's last day working for us. She's to be married this coming Saturday. She said to tell you 'hello', and hopes that the man you selected will make you happy. She also mumbled something about 'big hands' but I have no

idea what she was talking about. The social season is in full swing, although I dare say I have no interest in attending any party unless William will be there with me.'

The letter went on to recount what her mother had said about Mister Hildebrand finding himself a young woman to marry. Cassie also thanked her for the extensive wardrobe she'd left behind. Lily ran her fingers across the last few sentences.

'Perhaps, once William and I are married we can come to visit you in your new home and meet Mister MacKinnon. Or, maybe, the two of you could come here by train. I miss you, sister, but wish you all the best. Love, Cassie.'

"So, Lily, how were your letters?" Bren asked when he returned to the bottom step of the wrap-around veranda. "Did they make you miss your old life?"

Lily shuffled the papers into some semblance of order and stuffed them back into the envelope. "Not in least, Bren. If anything, they reminded me of why I left in the first place."

"What about your family?"

"Oh, I do miss them, of course. There's no reason they can't come to visit someday. As a matter of fact, my sister Cassie suggested it in her letter. Or perhaps, once we have adequate help here on the

Double L, we could go there. Maybe for my sister's wedding."

"Well, I'm not sure about leaving our homestead until we're well and truly secure, but your family is always welcome to visit. After all, we've built a house big enough to accommodate a dozen people. We might as well make use of it."

She offered her husband a saucy smile. When his gaze flared, she felt the now-familiar and most welcome flutters in the very pit of her stomach. She needed to get her mind back on their afternoon chores, not on the thought of making love with her husband.

"I'm going to check the coop for eggs," she told him, pushing herself to her feet. "I've left the instructions and all the loose parts for my new cookstove on the kitchen table. Perhaps, you could finish putting it together so we can prepare our evening meal inside tonight."

"I can do that, Lily," he told her, shooting a wink in her direction. "Right after I finish moving the last of the furniture crowding our parlor upstairs where it belongs. Especially, our new four poster bed."

"Yes, a comfy bed will be most welcome for a good night's sleep."

His chuckle followed her all the way to the hen house.

Chapter Thirteen

Southwest Cattle Auction
Union Hill, Texas
July, 1892

Lily made her way through the massive crowd of people walking from one barn to the next. Hay clung to the hem of her dress, despite the fact she'd gathered her skirt in her fists and raised it a modest inch or two off the ground.

Bren had already purchased a couple dozen head of fine beef cattle from the morning auction. Now, he was surveying the two pens of animals scheduled to go up for sale in the afternoon bidding.

She clutched her purse close to her chest as the cramped quarters caused more than one person to bump into her as they passed. It wouldn't do for her to lose the bank draft she'd brought to guarantee their purchases.

Bren, Billy, and Jerry Blackcrow were giving the last pen of animals a second look when she came to stand at her husband's side.

"How many more head do you think you'll be able to secure?" Lily asked.

"I'm hoping to get at least another dozen out of

this afternoon's bunch, and then another couple dozen, along with at least one bull, tomorrow." Bren confirmed.

"We managed to secure four wranglers to work the herd going back to the ranch," Billy explained. "Between Bren, Jerry, and me, we'll keep everything moving at a steady pace."

"We'll take turns driving the wagon," Bren explained. "That way you'll not be alone at any time."

"I'll have you know, I'm quite capable of handling our wagon," Lily protested. "Not to mention the fact that Hank and Teddy like me better than they do you fellows."

"I have no doubt of that, missus," Jerry told her. "You're much prettier than any of us."

Billy snorted a laugh. "For a city slicker, you do have a way with the animals, Lily."

Lily turned to Jerry Blackcrow. "I hope your lovely wife is finding everything to her liking back at the house. I truly appreciate her bringing her work out to the ranch so she could watch over everything for us."

"I'm sure she's in her glory," Jerry confirmed. "She's never lived in such a fine home before. No doubt, she'll be pushing me to build us something half as nice on the plot of town land that came with our storefront purchase."

"A home is important, especially once the children arrive." Lily spared a moment's thought for the time she'd spent holding Jerry and Amelia's little babe. "Arthur is a beautiful baby."

"He'll grow into a fine son," Jerry boasted. "I look forward to teaching him to hunt and fish."

"Yes," Bren added, "a son is a wonderful thing to have. You're a lucky man, Jerry Blackcrow. Lucky indeed."

Lily brushed her hand briefly across her middle and swallowed back her disappointment at the arrival of her monthly just two days earlier. While both she and Bren had agreed their focus needed to be on their ranch for at least the first year of their marriage, she felt certain he'd change his mind if she were to conceive.

Yet, so far, the was no baby on the way, but not for a lack of trying.

Bren stood up in the stirrups and stretched his back, before looking out over the open prairie. He could see two of the hired wranglers steering a few stray calves back to the herd. They'd ended up with seventy-two head of cattle, a mixture of calves and one and two year old cows and steers. The bull he'd purchased was being brought by freight wagon, along with two of the cows who were carrying late births.

Billy was riding in the wagon with Lily and, whatever he'd said to her, was causing her to laugh loudly enough to be heard above the noise of animals. Bren sucked in a breath. He trusted his wife, and Billy, but it rankled his nerves that another man was making his wife giggle like a schoolgirl.

Jerry and one of the other wranglers were driving the herd from behind, leaving him and fourth hired man to see to the left flank. He'd best keep his mind on the job at hand, Bren conceded. Otherwise, his herd might wander too close to the river than ran along their route to the north.

Despite knowing what must be done, his unwarranted jealousy sent his attention back to the wagon time and again.

"Time for you to get yourself back into the saddle," Bren said, pulling up next to the wagon and aiming his words directly at Billy. "You've had enough time lollygagging around."

Billy shot him a mock salute. "Sure thing, boss. Whatever you say." Drawing the wagon to halt, he jumped down and went to the back to untie his horse.

Once Bren had secured Duke at the rear of the

wagon, he climbed into the driver's seat at Lily's side. "How are you enjoying your first cattle drive, Lily?" Bren asked.

"Even with this parasol blocking out the sun, I'm wishing the canvas top you put back on the wagon extended out over my head. This heat is most unpleasant."

"We'll be stopping in another hour or so. We should be coming up on enough pasture for the animals, with a clear pond for them to water. And, thankfully, a copse of trees for us to set up beneath for the night."

"How much longer tomorrow?" Lily asked.

"If everything goes smoothly, we should be on our own land by mid-day."

"I must admit, I'm missing the comforts of our home."

Taking her hand in his, he gave her fingers a gentle squeeze. "Me too, Lily, me too."

Racing in a land run, claiming land, building a home, and establishing their ranch had been an unusual courtship, for certain. Yet, Bren realized he wouldn't have had it any other way. The trials and tribulations of their quick marriage and first few months had convinced him of a couple of very important facts.

He'd chosen wisely when he'd taken Lily Marie

O'Halloran for his wife. He also thanked the good Lord every day that she'd chosen him for her husband. And, most importantly, he'd fallen in love with his wife. Far more quickly than he'd thought possible.

It was half-past two the next afternoon when the back forty of their property came into sight. Bren breathed a sigh of relief. They were home, safe and sound, and in possession of all of their animals.

"Are you sure you won't hang around for awhile, Billy?" Bren asked when his friend pulled up on his horse. "Jerry and I could use an extra hand or two getting the herd settled."

"I promised pa I'd be home by the weekend. He wants to take his new lady friend to the wild west show they're bringing to Oklahoma City."

"Frank can manage, can't he?" Bren asked.

"I'm pretty sure that young girl he's been courting has her heart set on going to the show as well."

"With them both courting, you're going to be the odd man out soon enough, my friend," Bren joked.

"Fine with me," Billy responded. "I see you tripping all over yourself to please Lily. Not that she's not worth it, of course, but I got no desire to be tied down."

Bren reached across the distance between them and swatted Billy with the very end of Duke's reins. "Marriage is a blessing, Billy. I can't wait to see your stubborn arse fall."

Billy shook his head, his collar length hair shifting across the back of his sunburned neck. "Ain't gonna happen, Bren. Not in a million years."

Bren circled back to where the wagon trailed a few hundred yards behind. Lily was in possession of the reins and guiding the team as if she'd been born to be a rancher's wife. With this last stretch of land being so narrow, to avoid coming up on another homesteader's property all seven of the riders needed to be out in the open.

"Are you doing okay, Lily?" Bren asked when he pulled to her side.

"I'm fine, Brendan," she responded, the lilt of her voice filled with teasing. "I'm just pleased to see the back of our ranch coming up so quickly."

"Billy's going to ride ahead and open the gates. Steering this bunch through is going to be like threading one big needle. It might be best if you follow the road that runs along the end of the Hendrickson's place, and approach from the front."

"I can do that," she told him. "It'll give me a chance to say hello to Olaf and Gunter, if they're out and about."

"Don't visit for too long," he suggested. "I'm sure Missus Blackcrow will want to be relieved of her responsibilities soon enough."

"I agree. I'll be quick about it and meet you at the house."

Lily pulled the wagon to a halt on the road in front of the Hendrickson's property. Olaf was working along the front fence line and hanging their newly painted sign proclaiming the future home of O&G Farms.

"Good day, Olaf," Lily called from her seat atop the wagon. "Beautiful weather we're having today."

Olaf tipped his wide brimmed hat and strolled through the gate. "Afternoon, Missus MacKinnon. I see you've come back from the cattle auction. How did you and Bren fare?"

"Seventy-two head, with a bull and two bred heifers on the way."

"Sounds like a wonderful start to your ranch."

"Yes, it is. Have we missed anything important these past five days?" Lily wondered.

"Big stir in town yesterday for sure. The new list went up for those who either haven't improved and registered their claims, or those who have decided they can't cut it and want to sell."

"Anyone we know?"

Olaf nodded. "The Barrow couple on the other side of you are looking to sell."

"Really? Why? I thought they had their orchard all planned out."

"They're having irrigation problems. While they've got the creek that runs between your two properties, their back forty doesn't abut the tributary that runs into the Washita, so the land is dry. Shame too because they've planted all their saplings."

"Didn't they take the water into consideration when they claimed the land?"

The big man shrugged. "I think since they were only planning on planting on the front forty, they never gave the back forty a thought. Yet, it's sucking up at least half the natural irrigation."

"I'm truly sorry to hear of their troubles. I know they were quite excited at the prospect of planting their trees." Giving Mister Hendrickson a nod, she told him, "I'd best be getting home. Those fellows are going to be clamoring for a good supper after two days driving cattle."

By the time Lily pulled the wagon into the yard, Bren was there to unhitch the team.

"You go on in and get settled," he told her. "Missus Blackcrow has supper started but I'm sure she could use some help."

"I'll do that. However, after supper, I have something I want to discuss with you."

"Really? Should I be worried you've already found yourself a more suitable husband?"

"Don't be ridiculous, Bren. I haven't even been looking."

"So, that wasn't Billy trying to steal you away from me when he was making you laugh like a little girl?"

"Billy? Oh, heaven's no. He was telling me about the time the two of you were repairing fence on his pa's farm and you fell into the pigpen." Shooting him a grin, she added, "He says you stunk for a week."

"That I did, maybe even longer."

Chapter Fourteen

Supper that evening was a loud and boisterous affair, with not only Jerry and Amelia Blackcrow, but also Billy and the four men who'd traveled with them from Texas. "When will you fellows be heading back home?" Lily asked.

The tall, balding man named Phil swallowed back a mouthful of carrot and turnip mash and told her, "We're going into town for the night. Unwind a bit and rest our horses. Then, we'll head out in the morning. Without a bunch of slow cows to ride herd on, we'll be home before nightfall."

"I wish you safe travels," Lily told them.

All four men voiced their thanks.

Once the table was cleared and the wranglers had been paid and gone, Lily and Bren wished Jerry, Amelia, and baby Arthur a good evening and watched as they pulled away in their wagon.

"I'm taking off too," Billy told them. "Unless there's something you need me to do around here."

"Could you stay a few more minutes?" Lily asked. "There's something I want your input on, if you don't mind."

"Was that what you wanted to discuss after

supper?" Bren asked.

"Yes. Before I get into particulars, I was wondering about those water pipes you ran from the tributary to the end of the back forty. Could they be extended further?"

"Sure," Billy explained. "If we had the ironwork, we could run them all the way up to the house."

"Are you angling for running water, instead of a well?" Bren asked.

"No, not that I wouldn't welcome such a thing. However, I had another idea." She raised her head, meeting her husband's curious gaze. "Micha and Erralee Barrow are thinking of selling. They're having water problems. Their back forty, which they weren't going to develop anyway, is stealing all the irrigation from their orchard. Right now, all they have is our shared creek."

"And you're thinking we should run water to them?"

Billy scratched his whiskers and told them, "It's possible, with enough piping."

"I was thinking about a barter of sorts, assuming they truly want to make a go of their orchard," Lily explained. "We'd take possession of their back forty for more grazing land. In exchange, we'd cover the expense of running the water supply from our portion of the tributary to where their fruit trees begin."

"We could always use more grazing room, I suppose. Why don't we take a drive to their property in the morning?" Bren suggested. "We can talk it over with them. I got no qualms about sharing the Lord's bounty of water. However, I do want to take a look at that part of their land before I commit to anything."

Billy offered Bren his hand. "I'm out of here, Bren." Leaning forward, he buzzed Lily's cheek with a chaste kiss. "Keep this fella in line, you hear?"

"I hear," Lily confirmed. "I'll do my best."

Once everyone had left, Bren made his way around the first floor of their home and doused all the kerosene lamps while Lily checked to make sure the fire was out in her woodburning stove.

When they met at the bottom step, she eased her way into the shelter of Bren's waiting embrace.

"You know, Missus MacKinnon, you've got as kind a heart as you do a head for business."

"It's the Golden Rule, Bren. Do unto others as you would have them do unto you. I can't very well call myself a Christian if I'm not willing to help out my neighbor."

"Are you joking?" Micha Barrow asked, when she and Bren laid out her idea the next morning.

Turning to face his wife, Micha asked, "What do you think, sweetheart?"

"If it's possible to get water to our trees, I'm more than happy to give up the land we weren't planning to use anyway," Erralee confirmed. "I want so much to have our orchard, I'm willing to accept whatever solution works."

"How about we take a ride out and look at those back acres?" Bren suggested. "Let me get a feel for where we could run the piping and, of course, if what's there will be suitable for my cattle."

While the men rode out to the rear of the Barrow property, Erralee made tea and she and Lily retired to the parlor for a visit.

"Other than the water problem, how are you and your husband faring with this new adventure?" Lily asked.

"Obviously not as well as you and Mister MacKinnon. I truly wish we'd been as studious about choosing our lot as he must have been."

Lily nodded her agreement. "He had everything mapped out even before he reached Wichita for the run." Gazing out the window overlooking the yard, she added, "Your garden looks lovely though. And, from what I could see of your first fruit trees, they seem to be thriving."

"So far," Erralee confirmed, "but we can't keep

them watered fast enough. For all the rain we had on the way here, and those first few days, it's been as hot as fire, and as dry as a desert, this past month."

"Well, with any luck, Bren and I can help. What did you decide on for your orchard? Peaches and what else?"

"We're going to stick with stone fruits, for sure. Peaches and plums." Sighing deeply, Erralee explained, "It takes three to four years for the trees to begin producing properly. Fortunately, we brought some smaller trees that were a year old already. We'd also planned to order some trees to be shipped. However, just getting set up has been far more expensive than we imagined."

"Was that why you thought about selling out?"

"Yes," Erralee admitted. "Although, even just thinking about selling broke Micha's heart."

"It would have been the same for Bren if he'd not been able to get things up and running so fast."

"We cut a few corners building our cabin. I'd have loved to have a house as grand as the one you and Mister MacKinnon built, but it wasn't possible. Still, it's big enough for us and... God willing... a child or two in the future."

"It's a lovely home," Lily complimented. "Your husband did a wonderful job on the stone fireplace."

Erralee cast a warm glance at the opposite wall,

the hearth and carved mantel the centerpiece of the room. "Yes, he did, didn't he?"

The men returned an hour or so later, the two of them caught up in a discussion of weather patterns as they came into the room.

"Well?" Lily prompted once they stopped talking.

Bren gave a shrug of his shoulders. "It shouldn't take much to run the lines, that's for sure. There's a nice break in the trees where we can cut a clear path. As far as grazing land, about half of the forty will work for grazing. And, it is the section closest to our land, so there's that."

"And the rest of the acreage?" Lily wondered.

"Danged if I know what's wrong with it," Bren commented. "There's grass for as far as the eye can see, and then it stops suddenly and all you can see are a bunch of big brown patches of earth."

"I figure it's those darned patches that are soaking up all the water," Micha added.

"Assuming we cut this deal, I may try a few brands of seed to see what will grow. Or, maybe, call in a land expert," Bren told them. "In the meantime, though, if you two are willing to cut a deal, we can take that land off your hands."

Micha and Erralee exchanged glances. "Yes, we're interested. Our back forty in exchange for the irrigation pipe line from the tributary running through your land."

"Land seems like a lot to give up for a few old pipes," Lily said, drawing everyone's attention in her direction. "How much were you hoping to get for the farm?"

Micha shrugged. "I was gonna ask for two-bucks an acre."

"So, for the forty, that would be eighty-dollars," Lily confirmed. Giving her husband a smile, she suggested, "How about we make you an offer of sixty-dollars and the piping in exchange for the forty acres." Pausing, she added, "Of course, you'll also need to help with putting down the irrigation lines."

Bren pursed his lips and returned Lily's purposeful stare. "Seems fair to me," Bren acknowledged.

"Are you serious?" Erralee asked. "Money and the lines?"

"Yes," Lily said firmly. "That's our offer."

"We'll take it," Micha rushed to say. "We can draw up the papers and go to the land office together to make the transfer."

The deal made, Bren stood and offered Lily his hand. "We'd better be getting back to the house. I don't to leave Mister Blackcrow to do all the work."

"Yes, I have to water my garden as well," Lily

added.

"I can't tell you how much this means to us," Erralee told them.

Lily reached out and patted the other woman's hand. "It's what good neighbors do, Erralee. They help one another."

Once they were in the buggy and on their way home, Bren spoke up. "You didn't have to do that, you know. They'd have made the deal for the pipeline alone."

"I know," she said softly. "But, they're still a year or more away from their trees producing sellable fruit. They needed the help."

"Like I said last night, you're kind hearted, Lily MacKinnon. And I wouldn't have you any other way."

"Thank you. I wouldn't have you any other way than you are either, Bren." She took his hand in hers and squeezed. "Will you be able to get use out of at least most of the acreage? Other than those pesky brown spots?"

"I was thinking I might extend the fencing for a second field. That's were I'll put Charlie."

"Charlie?"

"That's what I've decided to name my bull." At her sideways glance, he added, "I was going to name him Arthur and call him Artie for short but, I suspect, Jerry and Amelia wouldn't appreciate me naming my bull after their precious little boy."

"Speaking of Mister Blackcrow, are things working out as you thought?"

"Even better. That man certainly has a way with the herd."

"Good, I'm glad."

Once Bren had drawn the buggy to a halt at the side of the porch, he jumped down and then reached for Lily, circling her waist with his big hands to lift her down. As always, just the feel of his warm touch, set her senses to reeling.

"You know, I could probably use an extra hand or two around here once things pick up. Maybe, for the winter, Micha might want to make some extra money."

Lily smothered a laugh behind her hand. "It would seem, Mister MacKinnon, I'm not the only one with a kind heart."

Bren drew her into his arms. Lifting her chin on his fingertips, he told her, "I love you, Lily Marie O'Halloran MacKinnon. I may not have said it before now, but I've felt this way ever since you walked into the meeting room back in Wichita."

She reached up and traced the line of his square jaw and feathered her thumb across his lips. "And, I love you, Brendan David MacKinnon. More than I ever thought it possible to love another human being."

"Our somewhat unconventional beginning has certainly turned out to be a blessing from God, hasn't it?"

"Yes, Bren, it has. But, then again, that's what happens when you have faith."

Chapter Fifteen

Summer gave way to autumn, the falling leaves creating a beautiful cascade of color across the front of their property. With Bren and Jerry Blackcrow out in the pasture tending to the animals, Lily busied herself with setting fires in the hearth, and in the huge woodburning stove in her kitchen.

Her kitchen. The realization still gave her a moment's pause. Another reason to thank the Almighty for her many blessings.

Both Amelia and Erralee had secretly been giving her cooking lessons, and Amelia had brought her a sewing basket and taught her how to mend.

If your mother could only see you now. Lily chuckled at her inner voice's prodding. No doubt Eleanor O'Halloran would collapse with a case of the vapors if she could see her eldest daughter wrist deep in the dirt of her garden.

The flames roaring in her stove, Lily took out the cast iron pot and set it atop the open burner, adding a large dollop of bacon fat, just as Erralee had shown her. Next, she added the meat the butcher had ground for her. A mixture of pork, beef, and lamb, the combination was sure to make her first attempt at a pot of chilli successful.

Taking Erralee's recipe from the wooden box on the shelf, she set to work.

It was half-past six, and far later than usual, when Bren entered through the kitchen door. Slapping his Stetson against the leg of his trousers, he placed it on the peg closest to the door.

"Hmm... something smells delicious." Sidling up to where Lily stood at the stove, he wrapped his arms around her and drew her backward into his embrace. "Is that chilli or did you put the wrong spices in the chicken and dumplings again?"

Lily swatted at his arm, then stroked the spot with the very tips of her fingers. Her touch made him hunger for something other than a bowl of chili.

"It's chilli. I used Erralee's recipe."

"Well, then, if it's half as good as hers, it'll be perfect."

She turned in his arms and shot him a narrowed glare. "I'll have you know, it's even better than Erralee's chili."

"That's a mighty boastful for a woman who couldn't boil eggs just a few months ago."

"What can I say? I'm a fast learner."

Bren bit back a laugh, the effort causing a

noticeable tick in his jaw. "You won't get any argument from me regarding all your new-found skills." Pressing a chaste kiss to her cheek, he told her, "I'm gonna go upstairs and wash up. I'll be back down in a couple minutes."

"Why were you so late?" Lily asked.

"The second calf was born earlier today. Stubborn little cuss decided to come breach, and the mama was having a hard time."

"Is everything all right?"

"Yep, between me and Jerry, we got the animal turned at the last minute. Mother and baby are doing just fine now."

Lily breathed a sigh of relief. "Thank the Almighty you and Mister Blackcrow were there."

Bren made quick work of his dirty clothes, washed his face and hands in the basin that sat atop the dresser, and then donned clean trousers and threw on a plaid shirt. He could hear Lily dishing up their meal and he had no intention of keeping her waiting.

Once he returned to the kitchen, he slid into the chair opposite his wife. She'd set out two bowls of some fine looking chili, a plate of biscuits, and pot of tea. On the drainboard next to the sink, he could see a homemade apple pie.

He released a long, weary breath. As tired as he

was, he realized there was nowhere else he'd rather be than here on this land, with this woman. "Shall I say grace, or would you like to do the honors?" Bren asked.

"Please, go right ahead."

Bowing his head, Bren recited a blessing from his childhood, finishing with an enthusiastic 'Amen'."

"Amen," Lily echoed.

Slowly, he lifted a spoonful of chili to his mouth, his gaze snagged on Lily's hopeful expression. The chili was just as he liked it, spicy but not mouth-burning, filled with lots of meat, and not too many beans.

It was—like his life and his beautiful wife—perfect.

After their meal was done and the kitchen tidied, Bren took Lily's hand in his and led her into the parlor. He needed to relax, to hold her, and revel in the beauty of their home, their marriage.

As soon as they'd settled onto the plush divan, Bren pulled Lily into his arms and nuzzled beneath the curtain of her luxurious hair. "You smell heavenly, darling," he mumbled against her throat.

"It's just my usual rosewater, Bren. But, thank you." Giggling, she admitted, "You smell a lot better than when you first came into the house."

"I have no doubt of that," he agreed. "So, tell me, Missus MacKinnon, to what do I own the honor of you fixing my favorite meal? Not just the chili and biscuits, but a tasty apple pie to boot."

She wiggled her way more fully into his embrace. As tired as he was, he knew if Lily gave any indication that she wanted to make love, he'd gladly oblige.

"I thought we should celebrate," she said simply, her soft words warming his heart, his soul.

"Celebrate?"

"Well, we have two new calves, don't we?"

"Yes, I suppose we do. Proud... what... surrogate parents to a couple of bull calves? No doubt, by next spring, we'll add even more to our herd."

Lily turned in his arms, and pressed a kiss to his cheek. "Actually, by next spring, not only will be adding to our herd, but also to our family."

Double L Ranch
Five Years Later
April 18, 1897

Bren stood up and surveyed the crowd seated around the three tables in his yard. Conversation moved easily between both family and friends, the occasional laughter causing heads to turn briefly at the sound.

Four-year-old Cody played off to the side with his best friend Arthur, the two boys running between the hedges in order to avoid Micha and Erralee's little girl. Yet, Susan held her own, despite the eighteen month age difference between herself and Bren's son.

Lily, his precious wife, sat in the rocker at the end of the table, baby Brianna nestled at her breast beneath the cover of a soft flannel blanket.

Raising his voice, Bren called out, "Can I have everyone's attention please?" The voices quietened, other than the random giggle from one of the children. "I'd like to welcome you all here today to help Lily and I celebrate our fifth wedding anniversary."

Claps and hollers went up all around before Billy Waters shouted, "I still can't believe Lily kept you this long."

"Never you mind," Bren scolded. "I'd also like to welcome our guests from Boston, my sister-in-law, Cassie and her husband, William Hildebrand. And, of course, our friends, Jerry and Amelia Blackcrow, Billy and Frank Waters, and Frank's lovely wife Millie. Also, our neighbors Micha and Erralee Barrow, and Olaf and Gunter Hendrickson."

"What about us?" Cody asked, tugging on

Bren's shirt sleeve. "We're here too."

"Yes, you are," Bren agreed, chuckling. "How could I forget? My son Cody, his best buddy Arthur, cutie pie Susan Barrow, and my adorable baby daughter, Brianna. And, of course, my beautiful wife Lily, and me… just Bren… your host for the evening."

Another round of applause went up, much to the children's delight.

Bren took his seat and lifted Cody onto the chair at his side. After Lily said grace, the food spread across all three tables was passed around from one person to the next.

A loving family, his own land, good friends, and faith. It was all a man truly needed. Tomorrow would be another day, another milestone. But, for tonight, they'd rejoice in all they had.

Once Lily put the children to bed, Cassie and William excused themselves and retired to their room. Billy, Frank, and Millie had taken off earlier, hoping to get at least halfway home before nightfall. The remainder of the guests—save for Micha and Erralee—left to make their way home.

As soon as the last guest was out of sight, Bren turned to his closest neighbors and asked, "Are you two excited for big day tomorrow?"

"Yes," Erralee responded quickly. "Imagine,

forming a joint partnership."

Lily stepped close to Bren's side and offered them all a smile. "I mean... who knew?"

Bren chuckled. "Obviously, not us. As far as Micha and I were concerned, they were just a bunch of brown patches that wouldn't grown grass, even with the finest seed."

Lily shook her head, as surprised as he was by this latest turn of events. "But... oil? I mean... what good is it anyway?"

"I'm not sure yet, Lily," Bren admitted. "According to the geologist we hired, it's going to make us rich beyond our wildest dreams."

"We're already rich, Bren. We have our family, our friends, our faith and, most importantly, we have each other."

The End

More Sweet/Inspirational Romance from Author Nancy Fraser

Ella: Prairie Roses Collection #4
Sweet/Inspirational Historical Wagon Train Romance
Will a widow's faith and determination allow her to trust again and make a safe home for her family, while welcoming the handsome marshal into her heart?

Avocado Toast
Sweet/Inspirational Contemporary Romance
Will Chloe's faith and determination help her lead Drew through his difficult decisions and bring them what they both need... a love that transcends their everyday challenges.

Once Upon an Angel
Sweet/Inspirational Romance
With a Touch of Fantasy
Novice angel-in-training, Ariel Pearce, needs to earn her wings. Will taking the newcomer along on her next assignment be just what she needs to succeed?

A Christmas Baby for Beatrice

An Historical Western/Inspirational Romance
Can a well-educated horticulturist and a widow find
the true happiness they both deserve in the wilds of
Washington State's pine forest?

An Honorable Man for Katarina

An Historical Western/Inspirational Romance
Can a women held against her will for six years
make a new life for herself and her children with the
help of the local sheriff?

Erin's Peachy-Keen Christmas

A Roaring Twenties Sweet/Inspirational Romance
Can a young woman displaced because of her party-
going friends find a new purpose with the widowed
solicitor and his young son?

Christmas Carole

A Contemporary Sweet/Inspirational Romance
Can a single mom of two turn the holiday grinch
into a believer? Or, will it take the magic of the 'wish
stick' to bring these two opposites together in time
for a perfect holiday?

Seth's Secretive Bride
Matchmaker's Mix-Up Series
An Historical Western/Inspirational Romance
She's looking for a professional man in California.
He wants a mature woman to help with his
emotionally-challenged son. What they get is each
other. Can the matchmaker's obvious mix-up be
exactly what they both need?

*All of Nancy's Sweet/Inspirational books are
available on **Kindle Unlimited**.*

Meet Author Nancy Fraser

Nancy Fraser a Top 100 best-selling and award-winning author. She was recently named Top Canadian Author for 2021 by N.N. Light's Book Heaven.

She's also the granddaughter of a Methodist minister known for his fire-and-brimstone approach to his faith. Nancy has brought some of his spirit into her Christian romances. And, her own off-beat sense of humor to her clean & wholesome books.

When not writing (which is almost never), Nancy dotes on her five wonderful grandchildren and looks forward to traveling and reading when time permits. Nancy lives in Atlantic Canada where she enjoys the relaxed pace and colorful people.